W0010279

SOMNIUM

(or, the Dream)

AND OTHER TRIPS TO THE MOON

EDITED BY JOHN MILLER AND TIM SMITH

CHRONICLE BOOKS

SAN FRANCISCO

Printed in Singapore.

Library of Congress Cataloging-in-Publication Data:
Somnium & other trips to the moon / edited by John
Miller & Tim Smith:
p.   cm.
ISBN 0-8118-1129-8
1. Science fiction—History and criticism. 2. Moon in
literature. I. Miller, John, 1959- . II. Smith, Tim, 1962-
PN3433.6.S66   1995
808.3′87620836—dc20   95-12956
CIP

Editing and design: Big Fish Books
Composition: Jennifer Petersen, Big Fish Books

Distributed in Canada by Raincoast Books,
8680 Cambie Street, Vancouver, B.C. V6P 6M9

10 9 8 7 6 5 4 3 2 1

Chronicle Books
275 Fifth Street
San Francisco, CA 94103

Thanks to

Kirsten Miller

Shelley Berniker

CONTENTS

E. E. CUMMINGS

Preface

HO KNOWS IF the moon's
a balloon,coming out of a keen city
in the sky—filled with pretty people?
(and if you and i should

get into it,if they
should take me and take you into their balloon,
why then
we'd go up higher with all the pretty people

than houses and steeples and clouds:
go sailing
away and away sailing into a keen
city where nobody's ever visited,where

always
    it's
        Spring)and everyone's
in love and flowers pick themselves

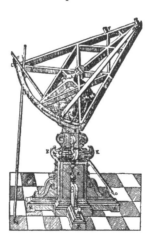

JOHANN KEPLER

Somnium

N THE YEAR 1608, when quarrels were raging between the brothers, Emperor Rudolph and Archduke Matthias, people were comparing precedents from Bohemian history. Caught up by the general curiosity, I applied my mind to Bohemian legends and chanced upon the story of the heroine Libussa, famous for her magic art. It happened then on a certain night that after watching the stars and moon, I stretched out on my bed and fell sound asleep. In my sleep I seemed to be reading a book I had got from the market. This was how it went:

My name is Duracotus. My homeland is Iceland, which the ancients called Thule. Because of the recent death of my mother, Fiolxhilde, I am free to write of something which I have long wanted to write about. While she lived she earnestly entreated me to remain silent. She used to say that there are many wicked folk who despise the arts and interpret maliciously everything their own dull minds cannot grasp. They fasten harmful laws onto the human race; and many, condemned by those laws, have been swallowed by the abysses of Hekla. My mother never told me my father's name, but she said he was a fisherman and that he died at the very old age of one hundred and fifty years (when I was three) after about seventy years of marriage.

In my early childhood, my mother often would lead me by the hand or lift me onto her shoulders and carry me to Hekla's lower slopes. These excursions were made especially around the time of the feast of St. John, when the sun, occupying the sky for the whole twenty-four hours, leaves no room for night. Gathering various herbs there, she took them home and brewed them with elaborate ceremonies, stuffing them afterward into little goatskin sacks which she sold in the nearby harbor to sailors on ships, as charms. In this way, she made a living.

Once, out of curiosity, I cut open a pouch unbeknownst to my mother who was in the act of selling it, and the herbs and patches of embroidered cloth she had put inside it scattered all about. Angry with me for cheating her out of payment, she gave me to the captain in place of the little pouch so that she might keep the money. And he, setting out unexpectedly next day with a favorable wind, headed as if for Bergen in Norway. After several days, a north wind came up; blown off course between Norway and England, he headed for Denmark and traversed the strait, since he had a letter from a Bishop of Iceland for

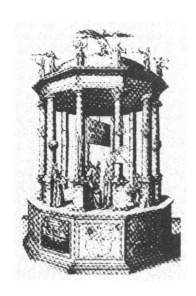

Tycho Brahe, the Dane, who was living on the island of Hven. I became violently seasick from the motion and the unusual warmth of the breeze, for I was in fact a youth of only fourteen. After the boat reached shore, the captain left me and the letter with an island fisherman, and, having given me hope of his return, set sail.

Brahe, greatly delighted with the letter I gave him, began to ask me many questions which I, unfamiliar with the language, did not understand except for a few words. He therefore imposed upon his students, whom he supported in great numbers, the task of talking with me frequently: so it came about, through this generosity of Brahe and a few weeks' practice, that I spoke Danish fairly well. I was no less ready to talk than they were to question and I told them many new things about my homeland in return for the marvels they related to me.

Finally the captain of the ship that had brought me returned. But when he came to fetch me, he was sent away. And I was very happy.

The astronomical exercises pleased me greatly. Brahe and his students passed whole nights with wonderful instruments fixed on the moon and stars. This reminded me of my mother because she, too, used to commune constantly with the moon.

Thus by chance I, who came from very impoverished circumstances in a half-barbaric land, achieved an understanding of the most divine science, which has prepared the way for me to greater things.

After I had passed several years on the island, I was seized with a desire to see my home again. I thought it would be no difficult matter for me, with the knowledge that I had acquired, to attain some high office among my rude countrymen. Therefore, after obtaining my patron's approval for my departure, I left him and went to Copenhagen. There some travelers who wanted to learn the language and the region took me into their company; with them I returned to my native land five years after I had left it.

I was most happy to find my mother still alive, still engaged in the same pursuits as before. And the sight of me, unharmed and thriving, brought an end to her prolonged regret at having rashly sent her son away. Autumn was approaching, and the nights were lengthening toward the time in Christ's natal month when the sun appears only briefly at midday before straightaway hiding itself again. During this holiday from her labors, my mother clung to me continually; wherever I betook myself with my letters of recommendation, she did not leave my side. She kept asking me, now about the lands which I had visited, and now about the sky. She delighted in the knowledge I had acquired about the sky. She compared my reports of it with discoveries she herself had made about it. She said she was ready to die since her knowledge, her only possession, would [now] be left to her son and heir.

By nature eager for knowledge, I asked about her arts and what teachers she had had in a land so far removed from others. One day when there was time for conversation she told me everything from the beginning, much as follows:

Duracotus, my son, she said, provision has been made not only for the regions you have visited, but for our land, too. For although we have cold and darkness and other inconveniences, which now at last I am aware of when I learn from you the delights of other regions, we are nonetheless well endowed with natural ability, and there are present among us very wise spirits who, finding the noise of the multitude and the excessive light of other regions irksome, seek the solace of our shadows and communicate with us as friends. Nine of these spirits are especially worthy of note. One, particularly friendly to me, most gentle and purest of all, is called forth by twenty-one characters. With his help I am transported in a moment of time to any foreign shore I choose, or, if the distance is too great for me, I learn as much by asking him as I would by going there myself. Most of what you have seen, or learned from conversations, or drawn from books, he has already reported to me, just as you have. I should like you to go with me now to a region he has talked to me about many times, for what he has told me is indeed marvelous. She called it Levania.

Straightaway I agreed that she should summon her teacher. It was now spring; the moon, becoming crescent, began to shine as soon as the sun dropped below the horizon, and it was joined by the planet Saturn, in the sign of Taurus, just after sunset. My mother withdrew from me to a nearby crossroads, and after crying aloud a few words in which she set forth her desire, and then, performing some ceremonies, she returned, right hand outstretched, palm upward, and sat down beside me. Scarcely had we got out heads covered with our robes (as was the agreement) when there arose a hollow, indistinct voice, speaking in Icelandic to this effect:

THE DAEMON FROM LEVANIA

Fifty thousand German miles up in the air the island of Levania lies. The road to it from here, or from it to the earth, seldom lies open for us. Indeed, when it does, it is easy for us, but for men the passage is exceedingly difficult, and made at grave risk to life. No inactive persons are accepted into our company; no fat ones; no pleasure-loving ones; we choose only those who have spent their lives on horseback, or have shipped often to the Indies and are accustomed to subsisting on hardtack, garlic, dried fish, and such unpalatable fare. Especially suited are dried-up old crones, who since childhood have ridden over great stretches of the earth at night in tattered cloaks on goats or pitchforks. No Germans are suitable, but we do not despise the lean hard bodies of the Spaniards.

The whole of the journey is accomplished in the space of four hours at most. For, busy as we always are, we agree not to leave before the eastern edge of the moon begins to go into eclipse. If the moon should shine forth full while we were still en route, our departure would be in vain. On such a headlong dash, we can take few human companions—only those who are most respectful of us. We congregate in force and seize a man of this sort; all together lifting him from beneath, we carry him aloft. The first getting into motion is very hard on him, for he is twisted and turned just as if, shot from a cannon, he were sailing across mountains and seas. Therefore, he must be put to sleep beforehand, with narcotics and opiates, and he must be arranged, limb by limb, so that the shock will be distributed over the individual members, lest the upper part of his body be carried away from the fundament, or his head be torn from his shoulders. Then comes a new difficulty: terrific cold and difficulty in breathing. The former we counter with our innate power, the latter by means of moistened sponges applied to the nostrils. When the first part of the trip is accomplished, the carrying becomes easier. Then we entrust the bodies to the empty air and withdraw our hands. The bodies roll themselves together into balls, as spiders do, and we carry them almost by means of our will alone. Finally, the corporeal mass heads of its own accord for the appointed place. But this spontaneous motion is not very useful because it occurs too slowly. Therefore, as I have said, we hurry the bodies along by willpower, and then we precede them, lest some damage be inflicted by a very hard impact on the moon. When the men awaken, they usually complain about unspeakable weariness in all their limbs; but they later entirely recover from this so that they can walk.

Many further difficulties arise which would be too numerous to recount. Absolutely no harm befalls us. For we stay in close array within the shadow of the earth, however long it is, until the shadow reaches Levania, when we disembark, as if from a ship. There we betake ourselves hurriedly to caves and to shadowy regions, in order that the sun, coming out into the open a little later, may not overwhelm us and drive us from our intended lodging and force us to fol-low the departing shadow. We are granted a truce for exercising our talents as the spirit moves us; we confer with the daemons of this province, and entering into an alliance with them, as soon as a place begins to lack the sun, we join forces and spread out into the shadow. If the shadow of the moon strikes the earth with its sharp point, as generally happens, we, too, attack the earth with our allied armies. This can be done at no other time than when men see the sun go into eclipse; it is for this reason that men so greatly fear eclipses of the sun.

So much for the trip to Levania. Now let me tell you about the place itself, starting, as geographers do, with those things which are determined by the heavens.

Although all of Levania has the same view of the fixed stars as we have, it has, nevertheless, such a different view of the motions and sizes of the planets that it must surely have a wholly different system of astronomy.

Just as our geographers divide the earth's circle into five zones with respect to heavenly phenomena, so Levania consists of two hemispheres: one

Subvolva, the other Privolva. The former always enjoys
Volva, which is to it what our moon is to us; while the
latter is forever deprived of the sight of Volva. A circle
dividing the hemispheres in the manner of our solstitial
colure [i.e., a circle on the celestial sphere which passes
through the poles and solstices] passes through the cos-

mic poles and is
called the divider
[because it divides
Subvolva from Pri-
volva, Kepler so
named the circum-
ference of the lunar
hemisphere that is
visible to earth].

I shall
first set forth the
features that are
common to both

hemispheres. All of Levania experiences the same succession of days and nights as we do, but in the year as a whole the people there lack our annual variation. For throughout Levania the days are almost equal to the nights, except that each day is by the same fixed amount shorter than the night for Privolva and longer for Subvolva. What variation there is in the course of eight years will be told below. Now at both poles the sun, balancing between day and night, circles around the mountains of the horizon, half of it hidden and half of it shining. For Levania seems to its inhabitants to be stationary, while the stars go around it, just as the earth seems to us to be stationary. A night and a day, joined together, equal one of our months, for, in fact, when the sun is about to rise in the morning, almost a whole sign of the zodiac is visible that was not visible the day before. And just as for us in one year there are 365 revolutions of the sun and 366 of the sphere of fixed stars, or to be more precise in four years there are

1,461 revolutions of the sun but 1,465 revolutions of the fixed stars, so for those on Levania the sun revolves 12 times in one year and the sphere of the fixed stars 13 times in one year, or to be more precise in eight years the sun goes around 99 times, the sphere of the fixed stars 107 times. But a cycle of nineteen years [the so-called Metonic Cycle] is more familiar to them. For in that number of years the sun rises 235 times but the fixed stars rise 254 times.

The sun rises in the centermost part of the region of Subvolva when the last quarter of the moon appears to us, but it shines in the centermost part of Privolva when the first quarter of the moon appears to us. These things that I say in regard to the middle regions are to be understood also with respect to the whole of the semicircles drawn through the poles and the mid-regions at right angles to the divider; you could call these the semicircles of the mediavolva [the central meridian of Subvolva].

Now there is a circle halfway between the poles that performs the function of our earthly equator, by which name it shall accordingly be called; it cuts in half both the divider and the mediavolva at opposite points; and the sun daily passes almost directly through the zenith of whatever places lie on this circle, and it passes exactly over it on two opposite days of the year, at noon. In the regions that lie toward either pole, the sun at midday declines from the zenith.

They have on Levania also some alternation of summer and winter, but this cannot be compared with ours in variety, nor does it always occur in the same places at the same time of year, as is the case with us. For it happens that in the space of ten years their summer moves from one part of the sidereal year [time required by the earth to make one complete revolution about the sun] to the opposite part, in the same location; for in the cycle of nineteen sidereal years, or

235 Levanian days, toward the poles summer occurs
twenty times and winter the same number, whereas
they occur forty times at the equator; they have annually six "days" of summer, the rest winter, correspond-
ing to our months of summer and winter. That
alternation is scarcely noticed near the equator
because there the sun does not deviate more than 5° to
either side of the zenith at noon. It is felt more near
the poles, since the regions there either have sunlight
or lack it in alternate half-year periods, just as is the
case on earth with those who live at either of the
poles. Thus the globe of Levania also consists of five
zones, which correspond in a certain manner to our
terrestrial zones; but the tropical zone extends barely
10°, as do likewise the arctic zones; all the rest are similar in extent to our temperate zones. The tropical
zone passes through the mid-parts of the hemispheres,
half its longitude, that is, through Subvolva, and the
other half through Privolva.

In the sections of the circle of the equator and the zodiac there exist also four chief points, as we have the equinoctial points [where the equator and ecliptic intersect—the ecliptic being the central line of the zodiac, the great circle of the celestial sphere that is the apparent annual path of the sun] and the solstitial points [where the sun reaches its most northerly and southerly distances], and from these sections the circle of the zodiac begins. But the motion of the fixed stars in natural succession from this beginning is very swift; since in twenty tropical years (years, that is, designated by one summer and one winter each) they travel through the whole zodiac, which happens with us but once in 26,000 years. So much for the first motion.

The calculation of the second motion is no less diverse in the case of motions which they see than it is in the case of motions that we see, and it is much more complicated. For all six planets—

Saturn, Jupiter, Mars, Sun, Venus, Mercury—experience, in addition to all the irregularities that are familiar to us, three others, two in longitude—one daily, the other in a cycle of eight and a half years—and the third in latitude, in a cycle of nineteen years. For in the mid-regions of Privolva the sun is larger when it is their midday than when it is their sunrise, other things being equal, and in Subvolva it is smaller; the dwellers in both areas think that the sun deviates several minutes from the ecliptic in each direction, now toward these and now toward those fixed stars. And these deviations have a pattern that is repeated, as I have said, in nineteen years. However, this wandering concerns Privolva slightly more and Subvolva slightly less. And although by the first motion the sun and fixed stars are considered as proceeding with even gait around Levania, nevertheless, for Privolva the sun at midday advances hardly at all in relation to the fixed stars, but to those in Subvolva it is very swift at noon; the contrary is true at midnight. And thus the sun seems to make certain leaps under the fixed stars, separate leaps on separate days.

These same deviations occur in the motions of Venus, Mercury, and Mars; in the case of Jupiter and Saturn they are almost imperceptible.

Yet this diurnal motion is not consistent at identical hours each day, but sometimes it is slower, both in the case of the sun and of the fixed stars, and then faster in the opposite part of the year in exactly the same hour of the day. And that slowness, making a complete circuit in the space of a little less than nine years, makes its way through the days of the year, so that now it takes place on a summer's day and now on a winter's day, which in another year had experienced swiftness. Thus, now the day, now in turn the night, is made longer by a natural slowness, and not, as with us on earth, by the unequal division of the circle of the natural day.

If the slowness befalls the Privolvan region in the middle of the night, an excess of night over day is accumulated, but if it happens in the day then night and day become more equal, which comes about once in nine years; the situation is reversed in Subvolva.

So much then for those features which are in a certain manner common to the two hemispheres.

CONCERNING THE PRIVOLVAN HEMISPHERE

Now as to the features that are unique in each hemisphere, there is great difference between them. It is not just that the presence and absence of Volva result in such different spectacles, but even the common phenomena themselves have very different effects in one region from what they have in the other, to such an extent that perhaps it would be more correct to call the Privolvan hemisphere nontemperate and the Subvolvan hemisphere temperate. For in Privolva

the night is as long as fifteen or sixteen of our natural days; it is gloomy with perpetual darkness, like
that of our moonless nights, for it is never illuminated by any rays of Volva; therefore, everything is
stiff with cold and frost, and there are besides very
strong, sharp winds; there follows a day as long as
fourteen of our days, or a little less, when the sun is
quite big and slow-moving with respect to the fixed
stars and there are no winds. Accordingly, there is
immeasurable heat. And thus for a space of one of
our months, which is a Levanian day, there is in one
and the same place heat fifteen times more burning
than our African heat and cold more intolerable
than of Quivira.

It must be especially noted that the planet
Mars, in the mid-regions of Privolva, in the middle of
the night, and in other Privolvan areas, each in its
own part of the night, appears almost twice as big as it
does to us.

CONCERNING THE SUBVOLVAN
HEMISPHERE

Passing over to this hemisphere, I shall begin with those who dwell on its border, that is at the divider circle. For it is peculiar to them that they see the elongations [angular distance] of Venus and Mercury from the sun as being much greater than we do. At certain times, even Venus appears twice as big to them as it does to us, especially to those who live near the northern pole.

But the most pleasant thing of all in Levania is contemplation of Volva, the sight of which the dwellers there enjoy in place of our moon, which is entirely lacking to those in both Subvolva and Privolva. And the Subvolvan region is so designated from the constant presence of Volva just as the other is called Privolva from the absence of Volva, because the dwellers there are deprived of the sight of Volva.

When our moon is rising full and advancing above the distant houses, it seems to us earth-dwellers to equal the circumference of a wine cask; when it ascends to the meridian, it displays the breadth scarcely of a human countenance. But when Volva is in the middle of the sky (a position it has for those who live in the very center, or navel, of this hemisphere), it seems to the dwellers in Subvolva a little less than four times greater in diameter than our moon does to us, so that if one

were to compare the two discs, Volva would be fifteen times bigger than our moon. But to those for whom Volva hangs perpetually at the horizon, it presents the appearance of a mountain on fire at a distance.

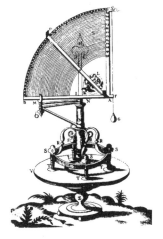

Therefore, just as we distinguish regions according to greater or lesser elevations of the pole (granted that we do not perceive the pole itself with our eyes), so the altitude of the ever visible Volva, differing from place to place, serves the same purpose for them.

For, as I have said, Volva stands overhead at the zenith for some, and for others appears low near the horizon; for the rest, it varies in altitude from the zenith to the horizon, but always, in any given place, the altitude is constant.

They also have their own poles, however; these are not at those fixed stars which mark our cosmic poles in the sky, but are in the region of other stars which are for us indicators of the poles of the ecliptic. In the space of nineteen lunar years, these poles of the moon-dwellers move in small circles around the poles of the ecliptic, in the constellation of Draco and the opposite constellations of the Swordfish (Dorado) and of the Sparrow (Flying Fish) and of the greater nebula.

Since these poles of the moon-dwellers are distant from Volva by almost a quarter of a circle, their regions can be marked off both according to the poles and according to Volva. It is obvious how they out-strip us in respect of convenience; for they indicate the longitude of places by means of their unmoving Volva, and the latitude by means both of Volva and the poles, while we have nothing for longitudes except that insignificant and scarcely discernible dec-lination of our compass needles.

For them, then, Volva stands in the sky as if fixed by a nail, and above it the other stars and the sun pass from east to west. There is no night in which some of the fixed stars in the zodiac do not betake themselves behind Volva and emerge again on the opposite side. However, the same fixed stars do not do this every night; all those which are within 6° or 7° of the ecliptic take turns. A cycle is completed in nineteen years, at the end of which time the first stars return to the place they had in the beginning.

Volva waxes and wanes no less than our moon, the cause being the same: the presence of the sun or its departure. Even the time is the same, if you look to nature; but they reckon in one way, we in another. They consider as a day and a night the time in which all the waxings and wanings of their Volva occur. We call this amount of time a month. Because of its size and brightness, Volva is almost never, even in its new phase, concealed from the Subvolvans. It is especially visible in the polar regions, which lack the sun at the time. There, at midday, Volva turns its horns upward. In general, for those living between Volva and the poles on the mid-Volvan circle, new Volva is the sign of midday, the first quarter the sign of evening, full Volva of midnight, the last quarter of sunrise. For those who have both Volva and the poles situated on the horizon, and live where the equator and the divider intersect, morning or evening comes with new and full Volva, noon and midnight with the quarters. From these examples one may take judgments also concerning those who live in between.

They even distinguish the hours of the day according to this or that phase of Volva: the closer the sun and Volva come together, the closer noon approaches to the former and evening or sunset to the latter. During the night, which regularly lasts as long as fourteen of our days and nights, they are much better equipped to measure time than we are. For apart from that succession of the phases of Volva of which we have said full Volva is an indication of midnight to the region of mediavolva, Volva itself also marks off the hours for them. For although it appears not to move at all from its place, unlike our moon, it nevertheless turns like a wheel in its place and displays a remarkable variety of spots one after the other, these spots moving along constantly from east to west. One such revolution, in which the same spots return, is considered by the Subvolvans as one hour of time, although it equals somewhat more than one day and one night of ours. And this is the only constant measure of time. For, as was said above, the daily journey of the sun and the stars around the moon-dwellers is irregular, as is shown perhaps especially by this rotation of Volva, if it were to be compared with the elongations of the fixed stars from the moon.

In general, as far as its upper, northern region, is concerned, Volva seems to have two halves. One is darker and covered with almost continuous spots, the other is a little brighter, with a shining girdle flowing between and dividing the two halves to the north. The shape is difficult to explain. In the eastern part is what looks like the front of a human head cut off at the shoulders, approaching a young girl with a long dress, to kiss her. She, with hand extended backward, is enticing a cat that is jumping up. However, the bigger and wider part of the spot extends westward without any clear shape. In the other half of Volva, the brightness is more widespread than the spot. You might say that there was the likeness of a bell hanging from a rope and swinging westward. What there is above and below cannot be likened to anything.

Not only does Volva in this way mark off the hours of the day for them, but it even gives clear evidence of the seasons of the year to anyone who is paying attention and who fails to notice the positions of the fixed stars. For even at the time when the sun occupies Cancer, Volva clearly shows the northern pole of its revolution. Appearing in the middle of the bright area, above the figure of the girl, there is a certain small dark spot, which moves from the highest and outermost part of Volva toward the east, and thence, descending into the disc, toward the west, from which extreme it moves again back to the upper part of Volva toward the east and so is then always visible. But when the sun is occupying Capricorn, this spot is nowhere visible, the whole circle, with its pole, being hidden behind the body of Volva. And in these two seasons of the year the spots head in a straight line for the west, but in the times between when the sun is in the east (that is, established in Libra) the spots descend or ascend transversely in a somewhat curved line. From this evidence we know that while the center of the body of Volva remains still, the poles of this rotation travel in a polar circle around their own pole once in a year.

The more diligent notice also that Volva is not always the same size. For in those hours of the day in which the stars are swift, the diameter of Volva is much greater, so that then it is more than four times as large as that of our moon.

Now what shall I say about eclipses of the sun and of Volva, which occur also on Levania and at the same moments in which eclipses of the sun and the moon occur here on the globe of the earth, but plainly for opposite reasons? For when we see the whole sun go into eclipse, Volva goes into eclipse for them; when, in turn, our moon goes into eclipse, the sun is eclipsed for them. Not everything matches exactly, however. For they often see partial eclipses of the sun when we are having no eclipse of the moon, and, on the other hand, they often experience no eclipse of Volva when we are having partial eclipses of the sun. Eclipses of Volva occur for them at the time of full Volva, as eclipses of the moon do for us at the time of the full moon. But eclipses of the sun take place at the time of new Volva as for us at the time of the new moon. Since they have such long days and nights, they experience very frequent darkenings of both heavenly bodies. Whereas with us a great part of eclipses cross over to our antipodes, their antipodes, which are in fact Privolva, see

absolutely nothing of these; the dwellers in Subvolva alone see them all.

They do not ever see a total eclipse of Volva, but they see a certain small spot, which is ruddy at the edges, and black in the middle, go across the body of Volva; this spot enters from the east of Volva and leaves by the western edge, taking the same course in fact as the spots that are native to

Volva, but surpassing them in speed, and it lasts a sixth part of their hour or four of our hours.

Volva is the cause of their solar eclipses, as our moon is the cause of ours; since Volva has a diameter four times larger than that of the sun, it is a necessary consequence that when the sun moves from the east, through the south behind the motionless Volva, and to the west, it very frequently goes behind Volva and thus the sun's body, either in part or as a whole, is hidden by Volva. The occultation of the sun's body, moreover, frequent though it is, is nevertheless very remarkable because it lasts several of our hours, and the light of both the sun and Volva is extinguished at the same time. It must certainly be an impressive thing for the dwellers in Subvolva, whose nights otherwise are not much darker than days on account of the splendor and size of the ever present Volva, when, during an eclipse of the sun, both luminaries, the sun and Volva, are extinguished for them.

Their eclipses of the sun have this singular feature which happens quite often; scarcely is the sun hidden behind the body of Volva when from the opposite side appears a shining, as if the sun has become enlarged and embraced the whole body of Volva, when otherwise the sun regularly appears so much smaller than Volva. There is, therefore, not always complete darkness, unless the centers of the bodies are almost completely aligned, and the arrangement of the transparent middle part [that is, atmosphere] allows it. But Volva is not so suddenly extinguished that it cannot be seen at all, though the whole sun hides behind it, except just at the mid-point of a total eclipse. At the beginning of a total eclipse, at certain places on the divider, Volva still shows white, as if a living coal remained after a fire has been put out; when this whiteness is also extinguished it is the middle of a total eclipse (for in a partial eclipse the whiteness remains), and when the whiteness of Volva returns (at opposite points of the divider circle), there comes a view also of the sun; so that thus in a certain manner both luminaries are extinguished at the same time in the middle of a total eclipse.

So much for the phenomena in both hemispheres of Levania: Subvolva and Privolva. It is not difficult to judge from this, even without my saying anything, how much the Subvolvan hemisphere differs from the Privolvan hemisphere in other respects.

For although the Subvolvan night is as long as fourteen of our day-night periods, nevertheless the presence of Volva brightens the land and protects it from cold. Certainly such a mass and such brightness cannot fail to produce heat.

On the other hand, though, the Subvolvan region has the troublesome presence of the sun for fifteen or sixteen of our days and nights; still the sun, being smaller, is not dangerously strong, and the luminaries in combination lure all the water to that hemisphere, and the land is submerged, so that very little stands up above water, while the Privolvan hemisphere, on the other hand, is dry and cold, since, of course, all the water has been drawn away. When, however, night approaches the Subvolvan area, and day comes to Privolva, since the luminaries are divided between the hemispheres, so also is the water, and the fields of Subvolva are laid bare, but moisture is provided to Privolva as a slight compensation for the heat.

All Levania does not exceed fourteen hundred German miles in circumference, only a fourth part of our earth. Nevertheless, it has high mountains, and very deep and broad valleys, and thus falls far short of earth in perfect roundness. Moreover, the whole of it, especially in the Privolvan tracts, is porous and pierced through, as it were, with hollows and continuous caves which are the chief protection of the inhabitants against heat and cold.

Whatever is born from the soil or walks on the soil is of prodigious size. Growth is very quick; everything is short-lived, although it grows to such enormous bodily bulk. The Privolvans have no settled dwellings, no fixed habitation; they wander in hordes over the whole globe in the space of one of their days, some on foot, whereby they far outstrip our camels, some by means of wings, some in boats pursue the fleeing waters, or if a pause of a good many days is necessary, then they creep into caves; each acts according to its nature. Most creatures can dive; all breathing beings naturally draw their breath very slowly; and, therefore aiding nature by means of art, they live deep down under the water. For they say that in those deep recesses of water, cold water remains, while the upper waves are heated by the sun, and whatever clings to the surface is boiled by the sun at midday and becomes food for the approaching swarms of wandering inhabitants. For, on the whole, the Subvolvan hemisphere is comparable to our villages, towns, and gardens; the Privolvan hemisphere is like our fields and woods and deserts. Those to whom breathing is more necessary introduce the hot water into the caves by means of a narrow canal, in order that, being taken into the innermost parts through a long course, the water may gradually become cool. They stay there for the greater part of the day, and use the water for drinking; and when evening approaches they go forth to seek food. In the case of plants, bark, in the case of animals, skin, or whatever may take its place, accounts for the major part of the corporeal mass, and it is spongy and porous; if anything is caught in the daylight, it becomes hard and burnt on top, and when evening approaches the outer covering comes off. Things growing from the soil, although on the mountain ridges there are few, are usually produced and destroyed on the same day, new growth springing up daily.

A race of serpents predominates in general. It is wonderful how they expose themselves to the sun at midday as if for pleasure, but only just inside the mouths of caves, in order that there might be a safe and convenient retreat.

Creatures whose breath has been exhausted and life extinguished through the heat of the day return at night, in a contrary fashion to the way flies do with us. For scattered here and there on the ground are masses in the shape of pine nuts, which have parched shells in the daytime, but in the evening, when the hiding places open up, as it were, they put forth living creatures.

The chief alleviation of the heat in the Subvolvan hemisphere is the constant cloudiness and rains, which sometimes prevail throughout half the region or more.

When I had arrived at this point in my dreaming, a wind accompanied by the sound of rain came along and dissolved my sleep and destroyed along with it the last part of that book obtained at Frankfurt. And so, having taken leave of the Daemon who was speaking, and of the audience, Duracotus the son with his mother Fiolxhilde, even as they had their heads covered, so I came to my senses to find my head in fact covered by a pillow, my body wrapped in bedclothes.

—*Translated by Patricia Freuh Kirkwood*

H . G . WELLS

The First Men in the Moon

I REMEMBER HOW one day Cavor suddenly opened six of our shutters and blinded me so that I cried aloud at him. The whole area was moon, a stupendous scimitar of white dawn with its edge hacked out by notches of darkness, the crescent shore of an ebbing tide of darkness, out of which peaks and pinnacles came climbing into the blaze of the sun. I take it the reader has seen pictures or photographs of the moon, so that I need not describe the broader features of that landscape, those spacious, ring-like ranges vaster than any terrestrial mountains, their summits shining in the day, their shadows harsh and deep; the grey disordered plains, the ridges, hills, and craterlets all passing at last from a blazing illumination into a common mystery of black. Athwart this world we were flying scarcely a hundred miles above its crests and pinnacles. And now we could see, what no human eye had ever seen before, that under the blaze of the day the harsh outlines of the rocks and ravines of the plains and crater floor grew grey and indistinct under a thickening haze, that the white of their lit surfaces broke into lumps and patches and broke again and shrank and vanished, and that here and there strange tints of brown and olive grew and spread.

But little time we had for watching them. For now we had come to the real danger of our journey. We had to drop ever closer to the moon as we spun about it, to slacken our pace and watch our chance until at last we could dare to drop upon its surface.

For Cavor that was a time of intense exertion;

for me it was an anxious inactivity. I seemed perpetually to be getting out of his way. He leaped about the sphere from point to point with an agility that would have been impossible on earth. He was perpetually opening and closing the Cavorite windows, making calculations, consulting his chronometer by means of the glow-lamp during those last eventful hours. For a long time we had all our windows closed, and hung silently in darkness, hurtling through space.

Then he was feeling for the shutter studs, and suddenly four windows were open. I staggered and covered my eyes, drenched and scorched and blinded by the unaccustomed splendour of the sun beneath my feet. Then again the shutters snapped, leaving my brain spinning in a darkness that pressed against the eyes. And after that I floated in another vast black silence.

Then Cavor switched on the electric light, and told me he proposed to bind all our luggage together with blankets about it, against the concussion of our descent. We did this with our windows closed, because in that way our goods arranged themselves naturally at the centre of the sphere. That too was a strange business; we two men floating loose in that spherical space and packing and pulling ropes. Imagine it if you can! No up nor down, and every effort resulting in unexpected movements. Now I would be pressed against the glass with the full force of Cavor's thrust; again I would be kicking helplessly in a void. Now the

star of the electric light would be overhead, now under foot. Now Cavor's feet would float up before my eyes, and now we would be crosswise to each other. But at last our goods were safely bound together in a big soft bale, all except two blankets with head holes that we were to wrap about ourselves.

Then for a flash Cavor opened a window

moonward, and we saw that we were dropping towards a huge central crater, with a number of minor craters grouped in a cross about it. And then again Cavor flung our little sphere open to the scorching, blinding sun. I think he was using the sun's attraction as a brake. "Cover yourself with a blanket," he said, thrusting himself from me, and for a moment I did not understand.

Then I hauled the blanket from beneath my feet and got it about me and over my head and eyes. Abruptly he closed the shutters and snapped one open again and closed it; then suddenly began snapping them all open, each safely into its steel roller. There came a jar and then we were rolling over and over, bumping against the glass and against the big bale of our luggage, and clutching at each other, and outside some white substance splashed as if we were rolling down a slope of snow. . . .

Over, clutch, bump, clutch, bump, over. . . .

Came a thud, and I was half buried under the bale of our possessions, and for a space everything was still. Then I could hear Cavor puffing and grunting and the snapping of a shutter in its sash. I made an effort, thrust back our blanket-wrapped luggage, and emerged from beneath it. Our open windows were just visible as a deeper black set with stars.

We were still alive, and we were lying in the darkness of the shadow of the wall of the great crater into which we had fallen.

We sat getting our breath again and feeling the bruises on our limbs. I think neither of us had had a very clear expectation of such rough handling as we had received. I struggled painfully to my feet. "And now," said I, "to look at the landscape of the moon! But!—It's tremendously dark, Cavor!"

The glass was dewy, and as I spoke I wiped at it with my blanket. "We're half an hour or so beyond the day," he said. "We must wait."

It was impossible to distinguish anything. We might have been in a sphere of steel for all that we could see. My rubbing with the blanket simply smeared the glass, and as fast as I wiped it, it became opaque again with freshly-condensed moisture, mixed with an increasing quantity of blanket hairs. Of course I ought not to have used the blanket. In my efforts to clear the glass I slipped upon the damp surface and hurt my shin against one of the oxygen cylinders that protruded from our bale.

The thing was exasperating—it was absurd. Here we were just arrived upon the moon, amidst we knew not what wonders, and all we could see was the grey and streaming wall of the bubble in which we had come.

"Confound it," I said, "but at this rate we might have stopped at home!" and I squatted on the bale and shivered and drew my blanket closer about me.

Abruptly the moisture turned to spangles

and fronds of frost. "Can you reach the electric heater?" said Cavor. "Yes—that black knob. Or we shall freeze."

I did not wait to be told twice. "And now," said I, "what are we to do?"

"Wait," he said.

"Wait?"

"Of course. We shall have to wait until our air gets warm again, and then this glass will clear. We can't do anything till then. It's night here yet— we must wait for the day to overtake us. Meanwhile, don't you feel hungry?"

For a space I did not answer him, but sat fretting. I turned reluctantly from the crater wall. These hummocks looked like snow. At the time I thought they were snow. But they were not—they were mounds and masses of frozen air!

So it was at first; and then, sudden, swift, and amazing, came the lunar day.

The sunlight had crept down the cliff, it touched the drifted masses at its base, and incontinently came striding with seven-leagued boots towards us. The distant cliff seemed to shift and quiver, and at the touch of the sun a reek of grey vapour poured upwards from the crater floor, whirls and puffs and drifting wraiths of grey, thicker and broader and denser, until at last the whole westward plain was steaming like a wet handkerchief held before the fire, and the westward cliffs were no more than a refracted glare beyond.

"It is air," said Cavor. "It must be air—or it would not rise like this—at this mere touch of a sunbeam. And at this pace. . . ."

He peered upwards. "Look!" he said.

"What?" I asked.

"In the sky. Already. On the blackness—a little touch of blue. See! The stars seem larger; the little ones and all those dim nebulosities we saw in empty space—they are hidden!"

Swiftly, steadily, the day approached us. Grey summit after grey summit was overtaken by the blaze, and turned to a smoking white intensity. At last there was nothing to the west of us but a bank of surging fog, the tumultuous advance and ascent of cloudy haze. The distant cliff had receded farther and farther, had loomed and changed through the whirl, had foundered and vanished at last in its confusion.

Nearer came that steaming advance, nearer and nearer, coming as fast as the shadow of a cloud before the south-west wind. About us rose a thin, anticipatory haze.

Cavor gripped my arms. "What?" I said.

"Look! The sunrise! The sun!"

He turned me about and pointed to the brow of the eastward cliff, looming above the haze about us, scarcely lighter than the darkness of the sky. But now its line was marked by strange reddish shapes—tongues of vermilion flame that writhed and danced. I fancied it must be spirals of vapour that had caught the light and made this crest of fiery tongues against the sky, but indeed it was the solar prominences I saw, a crown of fire about the sun that is for ever hidden from earthly eyes by our atmospheric veil.

And then—the sun!

Steadily, inevitably, came a brilliant line— came a thin edge of intolerable effulgence that took a circular shape, became a bow, became a blazing sceptre, and hurled a shaft of heat at us as though it were a spear.

It seemed verily to stab my eyes! I cried aloud and turned about blinded, groping for my blanket beneath the bale.

And with that incandescence came a sound, the first sound that had reached us from without since we left the earth, a hissing and rustling, the stormy trailing of the aerial garment of the advancing day. And with the coming of the sound and the light the sphere lurched, and, blinded and dazzled, we staggered helplessly against each other. It lurched again, and the hissing grew louder. I had shut my eyes perforce; I was making clumsy efforts to cover my head with my blanket, and this second lurch sent me helplessly off my feet. I fell against the bale, and, opening my eyes, had a momentary glimpse of the air just outside our glass. It was running— it was boiling—like snow into which a white-hot rod is thrust. What had been solid air had suddenly, at the touch of the sun, become a paste, a mud, a slushy liquefaction that hissed and bubbled into gas.

There came a still more violent whirl of the sphere, and we had clutched each other. In another moment we were spun about again. Round we went and over, and then I was on all fours. The lunar dawn had hold of us. It meant to show us little men what the moon could do with us.

I caught a second glimpse of things without, puffs of vapour, half-liquid slush, excavated, sliding, falling, sliding. We dropped into darkness. I went down with Cavor's knees in my chest. Then he seemed to fly away from me, and for a moment I lay, with all the breath out of my body, staring upwards. A huge land-slip, as it were, of melting stuff had splashed over us, buried us, and now it thinned and boiled away from us. I saw the bubbles dancing on the glass above. I heard Cavor exclaiming feebly.

Then some huge landslip in the thawing air had caught us and, spluttering expostulation, we began to roll down a slope, rolling faster and faster, leaping crevasses and rebounding from banks, faster and faster, westward into the white-hot boiling tumult of the lunar day.

Clutching at each other we spun about, pitched this way and that, our bale of packages leaping at us, pounding at us. We collided, we gripped, we were torn asunder—our heads met, and the whole universe burst into fiery darts and stars! On the earth we should have smashed each other a dozen times, but on the moon luckily for us our weight was only one-sixth of what it is terrestrially, and we fell very mercifully. I recall a sensation of utter sickness, a feeling as if my brain were upside down within my skull, and then—

Something was at work upon my face; some thin feelers worried my ears. Then I discovered the brilliance of the landscape around was mitigated by blue spectacles. Cavor bent over me, and I saw his face upside down, his eyes also protected by tinted goggles. His breath came regularly, and his lip was bleeding from a bruise. "Better?" he said, wiping the blood with the back of his hand.

Everything seemed swaying for a space, but that was simply my giddiness. I perceived that he had closed some of the shutters in the outer sphere to save me from the direct blaze of the sun. I was aware that everything around us was very brilliant.

"Lord!" I gasped. "But this—"

I craned my neck to see. I perceived there was a blinding glare outside, an utter change from the gloomy darkness of our first impressions. "Have I been insensible long?" I asked.

"I don't know—the chronometer is broken. Some little time. . . . My dear chap! I have been afraid. . . ."

I lay for a space taking this in. I saw his face still bore evidences of emotion. For a while I said nothing. I passed an inquisitive hand over my contusions, and surveyed his face for similar damages. The back of my right hand had suffered most, and was skinless and raw.  My forehead was bruised and had bled. He handed me a measure with some of the restorative—I forget the name of it—he had brought with us. After a time I felt a little better. I began to stretch my limbs carefully. Soon I could talk.

"It wouldn't have done," I said, as though there had been no interval.

"No, it *wouldn't!*"

He thought, his hands hanging over his knees. He peered through the glass and then stared at me. "Good Lord!" he said. "No!"

"What has happened?" I asked after a pause; "have we jumped to the tropics?"

"It was as I expected. This air has evaporated. If it is air. At any rate it has evaporated, and the surface of the moon is showing. We are lying on a bank of earthy rock. Here and there bare soil is exposed; a queer sort of soil."

It occurred to him that it was unnecessary to explain. He assisted me into a sitting position, and I could see with my own eyes.

●

ALMOST IMMEDIATELY we must have come
upon the Selenites. There were six of them, and they
were marching in single file over a rocky place, making
the most remarkable piping and whining sounds. They
all seemed to become aware of us at once, all instantly
became silent and motionless like animals, with their
faces turned towards us.

For a moment I was sobered.

"Insects," murmured Cavor, "insects!—and
they think I'm going to crawl about on my stomach—
on my vertebrated stomach!

"Stomach," he repeated, slowly, as though he
chewed the indignity.

Then suddenly, with a sort of fury, he made
three vast strides and leaped towards them. He leaped
badly; he made a series of somersaults in the air, whirled
right over them, and vanished with an enormous splash
amidst the cactus bladders. What the Selenites made of

this amazing, and to my mind undignified, irruption from another planet, I have no means of guessing. I seem to remember the sight of their backs as they ran in all directions—but I am not sure. All these last incidents before oblivion came are vague and faint in my mind. I know I made a step to follow Cavor, and tripped and fell headlong among the rocks. I was, I am certain, suddenly and vehemently ill. I seem to remember a violent struggle, and being gripped by metallic clasps. . . .

My next clear recollection is that we were prisoners at we knew not what depth beneath the moon's surface; we were in darkness and amidst strange, distracting noises; our bodies covered with scratches and bruises, and our heads racked with pain.

THE SELENITE'S FACE

I found myself sitting crouched together in a tumultuous darkness. For a long time I could not understand where I was nor how I had come to this perplexity. I thought of the cupboard into which I had been thrust at times when I was a child, and then of a very dark and noisy bedroom in which I had slept during an illness. But these sounds about me were not noises I had known, and there was a thin flavour in the air like the wind of a stable. Then I supposed we must still be at work on the sphere, and that somehow I had got into the cellar of Cavor's house. I remembered we had finished the sphere, and fancied I must still be in it and travelling through space.

"Cavor," I said, "cannot we have some light?"

There came no answer.

"Cavor!" I insisted.

I was answered by a groan. "My head!" I heard him say, "my head!"

I attempted to press my hands to my brow, which ached, and discovered they were tied together. This startled me very much. I brought them up to my mouth and felt the cold smoothness of metal. They were chained together. I tried to separate my legs and made out they were similarly fastened, and also I was fastened to the ground by a much thicker chain about the middle of my body.

I was more frightened than I had yet been by anything in all our strange experiences. For a time I tugged silently at my bonds. "Cavor!" I cried out, sharply, "why am I tied? Why have you tied me hand and foot?"

"I haven't tied you," he answered. "It's the Selenites."

The Selenites! My mind hung on that for a space. Then my memories came back to me; the snowy desolation, the thawing of the air, the growth of the plants, our strange hopping and crawling among the rocks and vegetation of the crater. All the distress of our frantic search for the sphere returned to me. . . . Finally the opening of the great lid that covered the pit!

Then as I strained to trace our later movements down to our present plight the pain in my head became intolerable. I came to an insurmountable barrier, an obstinate blank.

"Cavor!"

"Yes."

"Where are we?"

"How should I know?"

"Are we dead?"

"What nonsense!"

"They've got us, then!"

He made no answer but a grunt. The lingering traces of the poison seemed to make him oddly irritable.

"What do you mean to do?"

"How should I know what to do?"

"Oh, very well," said I, and became silent. Presently, I was roused from a stupor. "Oh, Lord!" I cried, "I wish you'd stop that buzzing."

We lapsed into silence again, listening to the dull confusion of noises, like the muffled sounds of a

street or factory, that filled our ears. I could make nothing of it; my mind pursued first one rhythm and then another, and questioned it in vain. But after a long time I became aware of a new and sharper element, not mingling with the rest, but standing out, as it were, against that cloudy background of sound. It was a series of little definite sounds, tappings and rubbings like a loose spray of ivy against a window or a bird moving about upon a box. We listened and peered about us, but the darkness was a velvet pall. There followed a noise like the subtle movement of the wards of a well-oiled lock. And then there appeared before me, hanging as it seemed in an immensity of black, a thin bright line.

"Look!" whispered Cavor, very softly.

"What is it?"

"I don't know."

We stared.

The thin bright line became a band, broader and paler. It took upon itself the quality of a bluish light falling upon a whitewashed wall. It ceased to be parallel sided; it developed a deep indentation on one side. I turned to remark this to Cavor, and was amazed to see his ear in a brilliant illumination—all the rest of him in shadow. I twisted my head round as well as my bonds would permit. "Cavor!" I said, "it's behind!"

His ear vanished—gave place to an eye!

Suddenly the crack that had been admitting the light broadened out and revealed itself as the space of an opening door. Beyond was a sapphire vista, and in the doorway stood a grotesque outline silhouetted against the glare.

We both made convulsive efforts to turn, and, failing, sat staring over our shoulders at this. My first impression was of some clumsy quadruped with lowered head. Then I perceived it was the slender, pinched body and short and extremely attenuated bandy legs of a Selenite, with his head depressed between his shoulders. He was without the helmet and body-covering they wear upon the exterior.

He was a blank black figure to us, but instinctively our imaginations supplied features to his very human outline. I at least took it instantly that he was somewhat hunchbacked, with a high forehead and long features.

He came forward three steps and paused for a time. His movements seemed absolutely noiseless. Then he came forward again. He walked like a bird—his feet fell one in front of the other. He stepped out of the ray of light that came through the doorway and it seemed that he vanished altogether in the shadow.

For a moment my eyes sought him in the wrong place, and then I perceived him standing facing us both in the full light. Only the human features I had attributed to him were not there at all!

Of course I ought to have expected that, only I did not. It came to me as an absolute, for a moment an overwhelming, shock. It seemed as though it wasn't a face; as though it must needs be a mask, a horror, a deformity that would presently be disavowed or explained. There was no nose, and the thing had bulging eyes at the side—in the silhouette I had sup-posed they were ears . . . I have tried to draw one of these heads, but I cannot.

There was a mouth, downwardly curved, like a human mouth in a face that stared ferociously.

The neck on which the head was poised was jointed in three places, almost like the short joints in the leg of a crab. The joints of the limbs I could not see because of the puttee-like straps in which they were swathed, and which formed the only clothing this being wore.

At the time my mind was taken up by the mad impossibility of the creature. I suppose he also was amazed—and with more reason, perhaps, for amazement than we. Only, confound him, he did not show it. We did at least know what had brought about this meeting of incompatible creatures. But conceive how it would seem to decent Londoners, for example, to come upon a couple of living things, as big as men and absolutely unlike any other earthly animals, careering about among the sheep in Hyde Park!

It must have taken him like that.

Imagine us! We were bound hand and foot, fagged and filthy, our beards two inches long, our faces scratched and bloody. Cavor you must imagine in his knickerbockers (torn in several places by the bayonet scrub), his Jaeger shirt and old cricket cap, his wiry hair wildly disordered, a tail to every quarter of the heavens. In that blue light his face did not look red, but very dark; his lips and the drying blood upon his hands seemed black. If possible I was in a worse plight than he, on account of the yellow fungus into which I had jumped. Our jackets were unbuttoned, and our shoes had been taken off and lay at our feet. We were sitting with our backs to the queer, bluish light peering at such a monster as Dürer might have invented.

Cavor broke the silence, started to speak, went hoarse, and cleared his throat. Outside began a terrific bellowing, as of a mooncalf in trouble. It ended in a shriek, and everything was still again.

Presently the Selenite turned about, flickered into the shadow, stood for a moment retrospective at the door, and then closed it on us, and once more we were in that murmurous mystery of darkness into which we had awakened.

Mr. Cavor makes some Suggestions

For a time neither of us spoke. To focus all the things we had brought upon ourselves seemed beyond my mental powers.

"They've got us," I said at last.

"It was that fungus."

"Well, if I hadn't taken it we should have fainted and starved."

"We might have found the sphere."

I lost my temper at his persistence and swore to myself. For a time we hated each other in silence. I drummed with my fingers on the floor between my knees and ground the links of my fetters together. Presently I was forced to talk again.

"What do you make of it, anyhow?" I asked humbly.

"They are reasonable creatures—they can make things and do things. Those lights we saw. . . ."

He stopped. It was clear he could make nothing of it.

When he spoke again it was to confess. "After all, they are more human than we had a right to expect. I suppose—"

He stopped irritatingly.

"Yes?"

"I suppose anyhow—on any planet, where there is an intelligent animal, it will carry its brain case upward, and have hands and walk erect. . . ."

Presently he broke away in another direction.

"We are some way in," he said. "I mean—perhaps a couple of thousand feet or more."

"Why?"

"It's cooler. And our voices are so much louder. That faded quality—it has altogether gone. And the feeling in one's ears and throat."

I had not noted that, but I did now.

"The air is denser. We must be some depth—a mile even we may be—inside the moon."

"We never thought of a world inside the moon."

"No."

"How could we?"

"We might have done. Only—one gets into habits of mind."

He thought for a time.

"Now," he said, "it seems such an obvious thing. Of course! The moon must be enormously cavernous with an atmosphere within, and at the centre of its caverns a sea. One knew that the moon had a lower specific gravity than the earth; one knew that it had little air or water outside; one knew, too, that it was sister planet to the earth and that it was unaccountable that it should be different in composition. The inference that it was hollowed out was as clear as day. And yet one never saw it as a fact. Kepler, of course—" His voice had the interest now of a man who has discovered a pretty sequence of reasoning.

"Yes," he said, "Kepler, with his *subvolvani*, was right after all."

"I wish you had taken the trouble to find that out before we came," I said.

He answered nothing, buzzing to himself softly as he pursued his thoughts. My temper was going. "What do you think has become of the sphere, any-how?" I asked.

"Lost," he said, like a man who answers an uninteresting question.

"Among those plants?"

"Unless they find it."

"And then?"

"How can I tell?"

"Cavor," I said, with a sort of hysterical bitterness, "things look bright for my Company."

He made no answer.

"Good Lord!" I exclaimed. "Just think of all the trouble we took to get into this pickle! What did we come for? What are we after? What was the moon to us, or we to the moon? We wanted too much, we tried too much. We ought to have started the little things first. It was you proposed the moon! Those Cavorite spring blinds! I am certain we could have worked them for terrestrial purposes. Certain! Did you really understand what I proposed? A steel cylinder—"

"Rubbish!" said Cavor.

We ceased to converse.

For a time Cavor kept up a broken monologue without much help to me.

"If they find it," he began; "if they find it . . . what will they do with it? Well, that's the question! It may be that's *the* question. They won't understand it, anyhow. If they understood that sort of thing they would have come long since to the earth. Would they? Why shouldn't they? But they would have sent something—They couldn't keep their hands off such a possibility. No! But they will examine it. Clearly they are intelligent and inquisitive. They will examine it—get inside it—trifle with the studs. Off! . . . That would mean the moon for us for all the rest of our lives. Strange creatures, strange knowledge. . . ."

"As for strange knowledge—!" said I, and language failed me.

"Look here, Bedford," said Cavor. "You came on this expedition of your own free will."

"You said to me—'call it prospecting.'"

"There are always risks in prospecting."

"Especially when you do it unarmed and without thinking out every possibility."

"I was so taken up with the sphere. The thing rushed on us and carried us away."

"Rushed on *me*, you mean."

"Rushed on me just as much. How was I to know when I set to work on molecular physics that the business would bring me here—of all places?"

"It's this accursed Science," I cried. "It's the

very Devil. The medieval priests and persecutors were right, and the moderns are all wrong. You tamper with it and it offers you gifts. And directly you take them it knocks you to pieces in some unexpected way. Old passions and new weapons—now it upsets your religion, now it upsets your social ideas, now it whirls you off to desolation and misery!"

"Anyhow, it's no use your quarrelling with me now. These creatures—the Selenites—or whatever we choose to call them, have got us tied hand and foot. Whatever temper you choose to go through with it in, you will have to go through with it. . . . We have experiences before us that will need all our coolness."

He paused as if he required my assent. But I sat sulking. "Confound your science!" I said.

"The problem is communication. Gestures, I fear, will be different. Pointing, for example. No creatures but men and monkeys point."

That was too obviously wrong for me.

"Pretty nearly every animal," I cried, "points with its eyes or nose."

Cavor meditated over that. "Yes," he said at last, "and we don't. There are such differences! Such differences!

"One might. . . . But how can I tell? There is speech. The sounds they make, a sort of fluting and piping. I don't see how we are to imitate that. Is it their speech, that sort of thing? They may have different senses, different means of communication. Of course they are minds and we are minds—there must be something in common. Who knows how far we may not get to an understanding?"

"The things are outside us," I said. "They're more different from us than the strangest animals on earth. They are a different clay. What is the good of talking like this?"

Cavor thought. "I don't see that. Where there are minds, they will have something similar—even

though they have been evolved on different planets. Of course, if it was a question of instinct—if we or they were no more than animals—"

"Well, are they? They're much more like ants on their hind legs than human beings, and who ever got to any sort of understanding with ants?"

"But these machines and clothing! No, I don't hold with you, Bedford. The difference is wide—"

"It's insurmountable."

"The resemblance must bridge it. I remember

reading once a paper by the late Professor Galton on the possibility of communication between the planets. Unhappily at that time it did not seem probable that it would be of any material benefit to me, and I fear I did not give it the attention I should have done, in view of this state of affairs. Yet. . . . Now, let me see!

"His idea was to begin with those broad truths that must underlie all conceivable mental existences and establish a basis on those. The great principles of geometry, to begin with. He proposed to take some leading proposition of Euclid's, and show by construction that its truth was known to us; to demonstrate, for example, that the angles at the base of an isosceles triangle are equal, and that if the equal sides be produced the angles on the other side of the base are equal also; or that the square on the hypotenuse of a right-triangle is equal to the sum of the squares on the two other sides. By demonstrating our knowledge of these things we should demonstrate our possession of a reasonable intelligence

. . . Now, suppose I . . . I might draw the geometrical figure with a wet finger or even trace it in the air. . . ."

He fell silent. I sat meditating his words. For a time his wild hope of communication, of interpretation with these weird beings, held me. Then that angry despair that was a part of my exhaustion and physical misery resumed its sway. I perceived with a sudden novel vividness the extraordinary folly of everything I had ever done. "Ass!" I said, "oh, ass, unutterable ass . . . I seem to exist only to go about doing preposterous things. . . . Why did we ever leave the sphere? . . . Hopping about looking for patents and concessions in the craters of the moon! . . . If only we had had the sense to fasten a handkerchief to a stick to show where we had left the sphere!"

I subsided fuming.

"It is clear," meditated Cavor, "they are intelligent. One can hypothecate certain things. As they have not killed us at once they must have ideas of

mercy. Mercy! At any rate of restraint. Possibly of inter-
course. They may meet us. And this apartment and the
glimpses we had of its guardian! These fetters! A high
degree of intelligence. . . ."

"I wish to Heaven," cried I, "I'd thought even
twice. Plunge after plunge. First one fluky start and then
another. It was my confidence in you. Why didn't I
stick to my play? That was what I was equal to. That
was my world and the life I was made for. I could have
finished that play. I'm certain . . . it was a good play. I
had the scenario as good as done. Then. . . . Conceive it!
Leaping to the moon! Practically—I've thrown my life
away! That old woman in the inn near Canterbury had
better sense."

I looked up, and stopped in mid-sentence.
The darkness had given place to that bluish light again.
The door was opening, and several noiseless Selenites
were coming into the chamber. I became quite still staring at their grotesque faces.

Then suddenly my sense of disagreeable strangeness changed to interest. I perceived that the foremost and second carried bowls. One elemental need at least our minds could understand in common. They were bowls of some metal that, like our fetters, looked dark in that bluish light; and each contained a number of whitish fragments. All the cloudy pain and misery that oppressed me rushed together and took the shape of hunger. I eyed these bowls wolfishly. It seemed that at the end of the arms that lowered one towards me were not hands, but a sort of flap and thumb, like the end of an elephant's trunk.

The stuff in the bowl was loose in texture and whitish-brown in colour—rather like lumps of some cold soufflé, and it smelt faintly like mushrooms. From a partly-divided carcass of a mooncalf that we presently saw I am inclined to believe it must have been mooncalf flesh.

My hands were so tightly chained that I could

barely contrive to reach the bowl, but when they saw the effort I made two of them dexterously released one of the turns about my wrist. Their tentacle hands were soft and cold to my skin. I immediately seized a mouthful of the food. It had the same laxness in texture that all organic structures seem to have up on the moon; it tasted rather like a *gauffre*, or a damp meringue, but in no way was it disagreeable. I took two other mouthfuls. "I wanted—food!" said I, tearing off a still larger piece. . . .

For a time we ate with an utter absence of self-consciousness. We ate and presently drank like tramps in a soup kitchen. Never before, nor since, have I been hungry to the ravenous pitch, and save that I have had this very experience I could never have believed that a quarter of a million of miles out of our proper world, in utter perplexity of soul, surrounded, watched, touched by beings more grotesque and inhuman than the worst creatures of a nightmare, it would be possible for me to eat in utter forgetfulness of all these things. They stood about us, watching us, and ever and again making a slight elusive twittering that stood them, I suppose, in the stead of speech. I did not even shiver at their touch. And when the first zeal of my feeding was over I could note that Cavor too had been eating with the same shameless abandon.

CYRANO DE BERGERAC

Journey to the Moon

HE MOON WAS full, the sky was cloudless, and it had already struck nine. We were returning from Clamard, near Paris, where the younger Monsieur de Cuigy, who is the squire there, had been entertaining myself and several of my friends. Along the road we amused ourselves with the various speculations inspired by this ball of saffron. All our eyes were fixed on the great star. One of our number took it for a garret window in heaven, through which the glory of the blessed could be glimpsed. Another, convinced of the fables of the ancients, thought it possible that Bacchus kept a tavern up there in the heavens and that he had hung up the full moon as a sign. Another assured us that it was the round, copper ironing board on which Diana presses Apollo's collars. Another that it might be the sun itself, having cast off its rays in the evening, watching through a peep-hole to see what happened on earth in its absence.

"And as for me," I told them, "I will gladly add my own contribution to your transports. I am in no way diverted by the ingenious fancies with which you flatter time, to make it pass more quickly, and I believe that the moon is a world like ours, which our world serves as a moon."

Some of the company treated me to a great outburst of laughter. "And that, perhaps," I said to them, "is just how someone else is being ridiculed at this very moment in the moon for maintaining that this globe here is a world."

But although I in-
formed them that Pythago-
ras, Epicurus, Democritus,
and, in our own age, Copernicus and Kepler had been of
the same opinion, I merely
made them laugh more
heartily.

Nevertheless this
notion, the boldness of which
matched the humour I was in, was only fortified by
contradiction and lodged so deeply in my mind that
for all the rest of the day I remained pregnant with a
thousand definitions of the moon of which I could not
be delivered. As a result of upholding this fanciful
belief with half-serious arguments, I had almost
reached the stage of yielding to it, when there came
the miracle—the accident, stroke of fortune, chance
(you may well name it vision, fiction, chimera or, if

you will, madness)—which afforded me the opportunity that has engaged me upon this account.

Upon my arrival home I went up to my study, where I found a book open on the table, which I had certainly not put there myself. It was that of Girolamo Cardano[1] and, although I had had no intention of reading from it, my eyes seemed to be drawn to the particular story which this philosopher tells of how, when studying one evening by candlelight, he observed the entry, through closed doors, of two tall old men. After he had put many questions to them, they replied that they were inhabitants of the moon and at the same moment disappeared. This left me in such amazement—as much at seeing a book which had transported itself there all by itself, as at the occasion when it had happened and the page at which it had been opened—that I took the

---

[1] *De subtilitate rerum* by Girolamo Cardano (1501—76), doctor, mathematician, philosopher, and alchemist.

whole chain of incidents to be a revelation sent in order that men should know that the moon is a world.

"How now," I said to myself, "here have I been talking about one thing all day, and now does a book, which is perhaps the only one in the world where this matter is so particularly dealt with, fly from my library to my table, become capable of reason to the extent of opening itself at the very place where just such a marvellous adventure is described, pull my eyes towards it as if by force, and then furnish my imagination with the reflections and my will with the intentions which now occur to me?

"Doubtless," I continued, "the two ancients who appeared to that great man are the very same who have moved my book and opened it at this page, in order to spare themselves the trouble of making me the speech they had already made to Cardano.

"But"—I added—"how can I resolve this doubt without going the whole way up there?

"And why not?" I answered myself at once. "Prometheus went to heaven long ago to steal fire there. Am I less bold than he? And have I any reason not to hope for an equal success?"

After these outbursts, which may perhaps be called attacks of delirium, came the hope that I might successfully accomplish so fine a voyage. In order to make an end of it, I shut myself away in a comparatively isolated country house where, having gratified my day-dreams with some practical measures appropriate to my design, this is how I offered myself up to heaven.

I had fastened all about me a quantity of small bottles filled with dew. The sun beat so violently upon them with its rays that the heat which attracted them, just as it does the thickest mists, raised me aloft until at length I found myself above the middle region of the air. But the attraction made me rise too rapidly and, instead of it bringing me nearer to the moon, as I had supposed it would, this now seemed to me more distant than at my departure. I therefore broke several of my phials, until I felt that my weight was overcoming the attraction and that I was descending towards the earth again.

My supposition was correct, for I fell to earth some little time afterwards and, reckoning from the hour at which I had left, it should have been midnight. However, I perceived that the sun was now at its zenith and that it was midday.

I leave you to picture my astonishment. It was very great indeed, and not knowing how to explain this miracle, I was insolent enough to imagine God had favoured my daring by once more nailing the sun to the heavens in order to illuminate an enterprise of such grandeur. I was further astonished by the fact that I completely failed to recognize the country where I found myself. For it seemed to me that, having gone straight up into the air, I should have come down in the place I had left from. However, accoutred as I was, I made my way towards a kind of cottage where I could see some smoke, and I was barely a pistol shot away from it when I found myself surrounded by a large number of stark naked men. They seemed greatly surprised to have encountered me for I was, I believe, the first person dressed in bottles they had ever seen. What still further confounded all the interpretations they might have put upon my harness was to see that I hardly touched the earth as I walked. What they did not know was that at the least impulse I gave to my body, the heat of the noonday rays lifted me up with my dew and if my phials had not been too few in number I could quite easily have been carried away on the winds before their eyes.

I was going to address them but they disappeared in an instant into the near-by forest, just as if fright had turned them all into birds. However, I managed to catch one of them, whose legs had doubtless betrayed his feelings. I asked him with some difficulty (for I was quite out of breath) what the distance was reckoned to be from there to Paris; since when, in France, people went about stark naked, and why they ran away from me in such alarm. The man to whom I was speaking was an olive-skinned ancient who first of all threw himself at my knees and then clasped his hands in the air behind his head, opened his mouth and closed his eyes. He mumbled between his teeth for a long time but I did not notice that he was articulating anything and took his talk for the husky babbling of a mute.

Some time later I saw a company of soldiery arriving with beating drums and observed two of them emerging from the ranks to investigate me. When they were near enough to be heard I asked them where I was.

"You are in France," they answered me. "But what devil has put you in that state and how comes it that we do not know you? Have the ships arrived? Are you going to inform my Lord the Governor? And why have you divided up your brandy into so many bottles?"

To all this I retorted that the devil had certainly not put me in the state I was in; that they did not know me for the reason that they could not know all men; that I knew nothing of the Seine carrying ships to Paris; that I had no message for my Lord the Marshal of the Hospital, and that I carried no brandy at all.

"Oho," they said, taking me by the arm, "so you want to play the clown. My Lord the Governor will know you all right!"

They led me towards their troop, where I learned that I was indeed in France—in New France.

Some little time later I was presented to the Viceroy, who asked me my country, my name, and my quality. I satisfied him by relating the happy outcome of my voyage and, whether he believed it or only pretended to do so, he had the goodness to arrange for me to be given a room in his house. My joy was great at meeting a man capable of lofty reasoning, who was not at all surprised when I told him that the earth must have revolved during the course of my levitation, since I had begun my ascent two leagues away from Paris and had come down almost perpendicularly in Canada.

In the evening, as I was going to bed, he came into my room and said to me, "I should not have come to disturb your rest if I did not believe that a person who can discover the secret of covering so much ground in half a day must also possess that of avoiding all fatigue.

"But you do not know what an amusing argument I have been having with our Jesuit Fathers about you," he added. "They absolutely insist that you are a sorcerer and the greatest compliment you can expect from them is not to be considered an imposter. Indeed, this motion, which you attribute to the earth, is a somewhat ticklish paradox. To be frank with you, the reason I do not share your opinion is that even if you left Paris yesterday, you could still have arrived in this country without the earth having revolved at all. For if the sun lifted you by means of your bottles, would it not have brought you here, since, according to Ptolemy and the modern philosophers, it travels in the direction you attribute to the earth? What great semblance of truth makes you judge the sun to be motionless when we can see it travelling? And is it likely that the earth revolves at such speed, when we can feel it to be firm beneath us?"

"Sir," I answered him, "here are the reasons, more or less, which oblige us to presume it to be so.

"Firstly, it is common sense to believe that the sun has its place at the centre of the universe, since all the bodies which exist in nature have need of this fundamental source of heat. It dwells in the heart of the kingdom so that it may swiftly satisfy the needs of each region. The first cause of all life is situated at the very centre of all bodies in order to function with equity and with greater ease. Wise nature has located the genital organs in man after the same fashion, pips at the centre of apples and stones in the middle of their fruit. The onion likewise protects, under the shield of the hundred skins which surround it, the precious seed whence ten million others must draw their essence. For the apple is a little universe in itself, wherein the pip, warmer than the other parts, is a sun giving off the heat which preserves the rest of its sphere, and the onion seed, according to this theory, is the little sun of its own little cosmos, which warms and nourishes the vegetative salts of this little body.

"If one supposes this, then I would claim that the earth, being in need of the light, heat, and influence of this great fire, revolves about it in order to receive in all its parts an equal measure of the virtues which conserve it. For it would be as ridiculous to believe that this great luminous body revolved round a speck, which is useless to it, as to imagine when we see a roast lark, that the hearth has been revolved about it in order to cook it. Otherwise, if the sun had to perform this task, it would seem as if the medicine needed the sick man, the strong should yield to the weak, the great serve the small and, instead of a ship sailing along the shores of a province, the province would have to be navigated round the ship. And if you find it difficult to understand how such a heavy mass can move, I pray you tell me if the stars and the heavens, which you would have so solid, are any lighter? Since we are certain of the rotundity of the earth, it is easy for us to deduce its motion from its shape. But why should you suppose the sky to be round, since you cannot know for sure? And if, out of all the possible shapes, it does not happen to possess this one, it is certain that it cannot move.

"I am not going to reproach you for your *eccentrics*, your *concentrics*, and your *epicycles*, all of which you could only explain very confusedly and from which

I have rescued my own system. Let us simply discuss the natural causes of this motion. *You* are all forced to fall back on intelligences which move and govern your spheres. But I, on the other hand, do not disturb the repose of the Supreme Being, who doubtless created nature all perfect, and who is wise enough to have accomplished the task in such a way that, having made it complete in one respect, He did not leave it defective in another. I, I tell you, find in the earth itself the virtues which make it move. I maintain that the rays and influences of the sun fall upon it as they circulate and make it revolve (just as we make a globe revolve by striking it with our hands); or equally that the vapours continually evaporating from its heart on the side visible to the sun are repelled by the cold of the middle region of the air and fall back upon it, and, of necessity only being able to strike at an angle, thus make it pirouette.

"The explanation of the other two motions is even less complicated. Pray you, consider a little. . . ."

At these words the Viceroy interrupted me: "I would prefer," he said, "to spare you the trouble, since I have read several books by Gassendi on this subject, but on condition that you listen to the reply given me one day by one of our Fathers who was upholding your opinion. 'Indeed,' he said, 'I am convinced that the earth revolves, not for the reasons alleged by Copernicus, but because the fires of hell, as the Holy Scriptures tell us, are enclosed in the centre of the earth and the damned, seeking to escape the burning flames, clamber up the vault in order to avoid them and thus cause the earth to revolve, as a dog turns a wheel when it runs enclosed within it.'"

We spent some time praising this notion as a pure fruit of the good Father's zeal, and finally the Viceroy told me he was much astonished, seeing how improbable Ptolemy's system was, that it should have been so generally accepted.

"Sir," I replied to him, "the majority of men,

who only judge things by their senses, have allowed themselves to be persuaded by their eyes, and just as the man on board a ship which hugs the coastline believes that he is motionless and the shore is moving, so have men, revolving with the earth about the sky, believed that it was the sky itself which revolved about them. Added to this there is the intolerable pride of human beings, who are convinced that nature was only made for them—as if it were likely that the sun, a vast body four hundred and thirty-four times greater than the earth, should only have been set ablaze in order to ripen their medlars and to make their cabbages grow heads!

"As for me, far from agreeing with their impudence, I believe that the planets are worlds surrounding the sun and the fixed stars are also suns with planets surrounding them; that is to say, worlds which we cannot see from here, on account of their smallness, and because their light, being borrowed, cannot reach us. For how, in good faith, can one imagine these globes of

such magnitude to be nothing but great desert coun-
tries, while ours, simply because we, a handful of vain-
glorious ruffians are crawling about on it, has been made
to command all the others? What! Just because the sun
charts our days and years for us, does that mean to say it
was only made to stop us banging our heads against the
walls? No, no, if this visible god lights man's way it is by
accident, as the King's torch accidentally gives light to
the passing street-porter."

"But," he said to me, "if, as you affirm, the
fixed stars are so many suns, one could conclude from
this that the universe is infinite, since it is likely that the
peoples of one of these worlds going round a fixed star
can themselves observe other fixed stars, farther above
them, which we cannot make out from here, and so on,
to infinity."

"Without a doubt," I replied. "Just as God
could make the soul immortal, so He could make the
universe infinite, if it be true that eternity is nothing

but an endless duration of time and infinity a limitless stretch of space. Besides, if the universe were not infinite, God Himself would be finite, since He could not exist where there was nothing. In that case, He could not increase the size of the universe without adding something to His own dimensions and beginning to exist where He had not been before. One must therefore believe that, just as we can see Saturn and Jupiter from here, if we were on one or other of them we should discover many worlds which we cannot now perceive, and that the cosmos is constructed in this way to infinity."

"Upon my soul!" he replied to me, "it is no use your talking so. I shall never understand this infinity."

"Why! tell me," I countered, "do you understand the nothingness beyond the end of space? Not at all! For when you think about this nothingness, at the very least you imagine it like wind, or like air—and that is something. But even if you do not understand infinity as a whole you may at least conceive of it in parts, since it is not difficult to picture, beyond the earth, air, and fire which we can see, more air and more earth. And infinity is really nothing but a limitless texture of all that. And if you ask me in what manner these worlds were made, seeing that the Holy Scripture tells us only of the one which God created, I reply that it only speaks of ours for the reason that it is the only one which God wished to take the trouble of making with His own hands, while all the others we see, or do not see, suspended amidst the azure of the cosmos, are nothing but the dross of suns purging themselves. For how could these great fires subsist if they were not attached to some matter which feeds them? So, just as fire expels the cinders which choke it, and gold, when it is refined in the crucible, divides from the marcasite which weakens its carat, and we vomit to free our hearts of the indigestible humours which attack them, so these suns disgorge and purge themselves every day of the remains

of the matter which is the
fuel for their fire. But when
they have burned up all the
matter which sustains them,
they will scatter in every
direction, you need have no
doubt, in search of fresh
nourishment, and they will
attach themselves to all the

worlds they formerly created, particularly the nearest
to hand. And so these great fires will mix all the bodies
up together again and then drive them out everywhere
pell-mell, as before, and, having little by little purified
themselves, they will begin to serve as suns for other little worlds, which they engender by expelling them out
of their own spheres.

"And that is doubtless what made the
Pythagoreans predict universal conflagration. This is
not a ridiculous fancy: New France, where we are, pro-

vides a convincing example of it. This vast continent of America forms a half of the earth which, despite our ancestors having sailed the ocean a thousand times, had never been discovered. It is evident that it was not yet there; nor were many of the islands, peninsulas, and mountains which have since appeared on our globe, when the dross from the sun, as it purged itself, was driven far enough and condensed in clusters heavy enough to be attracted by the centre of our earth—possibly little by little, in tiny particles, perhaps all at once in a mass. This theory is not so unreasonable that Saint Augustin would not have applauded it, if the discovery of this continent had been made in his time, for this great man, whose genius was enlightened by the Holy Spirit, affirms that in his time the earth was as flat as a pancake and floated upon the water like half a sliced orange.

"But if ever I have the honour of seeing you in France, I will show you, with the aid of an excellent spy-glass, that certain obscurities, which look like spots from here, are worlds in formation."

My eyes were closing as I finished this speech and the Viceroy was obliged to leave me. On the next day and the days following we had conversations of a similar nature. But when some time later the pressure of the affairs of the province called a halt to our philoso-phizing, I returned even more eagerly to my intention of ascending to the moon.

As soon as it rose I would go off through the woods, dreaming of the conduct and success of my enterprise; and, finally, one Eve of St. John, when a council was being held at the Fort to determine whether help should be given to the local savages against the Iroquois, I went off all alone behind our house to the top of a small hill and here is what I carried out. I had built a machine which I imagined capable of lifting me as high as I desired and in my opinion it lacked nothing essential. I seated myself inside it and launched myself into the air from the top of a rock. But because my preparations had been inadequate I tumbled roughly into the valley. Covered with bruises as I was, I nevertheless returned from there to my room without losing heart, took some marrow of beef and anointed my whole body with it, for I was battered all over from head to foot. After fortifying my courage with a bottle of a cordial essence, I returned to look for my machine. I did not find it, however, for some soldiers, who had been sent into the forest to cut wood to build a fire for the feast of St. John, had chanced upon it and brought it to the Fort, where several explanations of what it could be were advanced. When the device of the spring was discovered, some said a quantity of rockets should be attached to it, so that when their speed had lifted them high enough and the motor was agitating its great wings, no one could fail to take the machine for a fire dragon.

Meanwhile I spent a long time searching for it, but at last I found it in the middle of the square in Quebec just as they were setting fire to it. My dismay at discovering my handiwork in such danger so excited me that I ran to seize the arm of the soldier who was setting light to it. I snatched the fuse from him and threw myself furiously into my machine to destroy the contrivance with which it had been surrounded, but I arrived too late, for I had hardly set my two feet inside it when I was borne up into the blue.

The horror which overcame me did not destroy my presence of mind so completely as to make me incapable of recalling later what happened to me at that moment. When the fire had consumed one row of the rockets, which had been arranged six by six, the device of a fuse, fixed at the end of each half dozen, set off another layer and then another, so that the saltpetre caught fire and gave me a fresh lease of life, at the same time as it carried me farther into danger.

However, when the supply was all used up, the contrivance failed and I was resigning myself to leaving my crown upon that of some mountain when (without my making any movement at all) I felt my levitation continuing. My machine took leave of me and I saw it falling back towards the earth. This extraordinary occurrence filled my heart with a joy so uncommon that in my delight at seeing myself delivered from certain disaster, I had the impudence to philosophize upon it. As I was thus exercising my eyes and my brain to seek out the cause, I noticed my swollen flesh, still greasy with the marrow I had smeared upon myself for the bruises from my tumble. I realized that the moon was on the wane and, just as it is accustomed in that quarter to suck the marrow out of animals,[2] so it was drinking up what I had smeared upon myself, and with all the more strength because its globe was nearer to me, so that its vigour was in no way impaired by the intervention of clouds.

---

[2] It was popularly believed that, when the moon was on the wane, the bones of animals contained little or no marrow, since it was sucked out of them by the moon.

When, according to the calculations I have since made, I had travelled much more than three quarters of the way from the earth to the moon, I suddenly found myself falling head first, although I had not somersaulted in any fashion. I would not, indeed, have noticed this, if I had not felt my head taking the weight of my body. I was, in fact, quite certain that I was not falling back towards our world, for although I found myself between two moons, I could clearly observe that the farther I went from one, the nearer I came to the other, and I was convinced that the larger one was our globe, since, after I had been travelling for a day or two, the reflected light of the sun grew more distant and gradually the distinctions between different land masses and climates became blurred and it no longer seemed to me like anything other than a great disc of gold. This made me think I was coming down towards the moon and this supposition was confirmed when I came to remember that I had only begun to fall after three quarters of the way.

"For," I said to myself, "this body, being smaller than our earth, must have a less extensive sphere of influence and in consequence I have felt the pull of its centre later."

At last, after I had been falling for a very long time—or so I presumed, for the violence of my precipitation made observation diffi-cult—the next thing I can remember is finding myself under a tree, entangled with two or three large branches which I had shattered in my fall, and with my face moist from an apple which had been crushed against it.

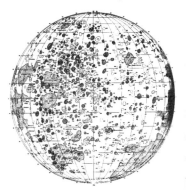

—Translated by Geoffrey Strachen

LUCIAN

The True History

ONCE SET sail from Gibraltar with
a brisk wind behind me and steered
westward into the Atlantic. My rea-
son for doing so? Mere curiosity. I just felt I needed a
change, and wanted to find out what happened the
other side of the Ocean, and what sort of people lived
there. With this object in view I had taken on board an
enormous supply of food and water, and collected fifty
other young men who felt the same way as I did to
keep me company. I had also provided all the weapons
that we could possibly need, hired the best steersman

available (at an exorbitant wage) and had our ship, which was only a light craft, specially reinforced to withstand the stresses and strains of a long voyage.

After sailing along at a moderate speed for twenty-four hours, we were still within sight of land; but at dawn the following day the wind increased to gale-force, the waves rose mountain-high, the sky grew black as night and it became impossible even to take in sail. There was nothing we could do but let her run before the wind and hope for the best.

The storm went on for seventy-nine days, but on the eightieth the sun suddenly shone through and revealed an island not far off. It was hilly and cov- ered with trees, and now that the worst of the storm was over, the roar of the waves breaking against the shore had died down to a soft murmur. So we landed and threw ourselves down, utterly exhausted, on the sand. After all we had been through, you can imagine how long we lay there; but eventually we got up, and leaving thirty men to guard the ship, I and the other twenty went off to explore the island.

We started walking inland through the woods, and when we had gone about six hundred yards we came across a bronze tablet with a Greek inscription on it. The letters were almost worn away, but we just managed to make out the words: "Hercules and Dionysus got this far." We also spotted a couple of footprints on a rock nearby, one about a hundred feet long, and the other, I should say, about ninety-nine. Presumably Hercules has somewhat larger feet than Dionysus.

We sank reverently to our knees and said a prayer. Then we went on a bit further and came to a river of wine, which tasted exactly like Chianti. It was deep enough in places to float a battleship, and any doubts we might have had about the authenticity of the inscription were immediately dispelled. Dionysus had been there all right!

I was curious to know where the river came from, so I walked up-stream until I arrived at the source, which was of a most unusual kind. It consisted of a group of giant vines, loaded with enormous grapes. From the root of each plant trickled sparkling drops of wine, which eventually converged to form the river. There were lots of wine-coloured fish swimming about in it, and they tasted like wine too, for we caught and ate some, and they made us extremely drunk. Needless to say, when we cut them open we found they were full of wine-lees. Later, we hit on the idea of diluting them with ordinary water-fish and thus reducing the alcoholic content of our food.

After lunch we waded across the river at one of the shallower spots, and came upon some specimens of a very rare type of vine. They had good thick trunks growing out of the ground in the normal manner, but apart from that they were women, complete in every detail from the waist upwards. In fact they

were exactly like those pictures you see of Daphne
being turned into a tree just
as Apollo is about to catch
her. From the tips of their
fingers sprouted vine-shoots
loaded with grapes, and their
hair consisted of vine-leaves
and tendrils.

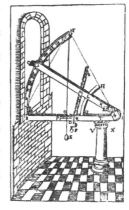

When we went up to them, they shook us
warmly by the hand and said they were delighted to
see us, some saying it in Lydian, some in Hindustani,
but most of them in Greek. Then they wanted us to
kiss them, and every man who put his lips to theirs
got very drunk and started lurching about. They
would not allow us to pick their fruit, and shrieked
with pain when anyone tried to do so; but they were
more than willing to be deflowered, and two of us
who volunteered to oblige them found it quite

impossible to withdraw from their engagements afterwards. They became literally rooted to the spot, their
fingers turning into vine-shoots and their hair into
tendrils, and looked like having little grapes of their
own at any moment.

So we left them to their fate and ran back to
the ship, where we told the others what we had seen
and described the results of the experiment in cross-
fertilisation. Then we went off again with buckets to
replenish our water-supply, and while we were about
it, to restock our cellar from the river. After that we
spent the night on the beach beside our ship, and next
morning put to sea with a gentle breeze behind us.

About mid-day, when we had already lost
sight of the island, we were suddenly hit by a typhoon,
which whirled the ship round at an appalling speed
and lifted it to a height of approximately 1,800,000
feet. While we were up there, a powerful wind caught
our sails and bellied them out, so instead of falling back

on to the sea we continued to sail through the air for the next seven days—and, of course, an equal number of nights. On the eighth day we sighted what looked like a big island hanging in mid-air, white and round and brilliantly illuminated, so we steered towards it, dropped anchor and disembarked.

A brief reconnaissance was enough to tell us that the country was inhabited and under cultivation, and so long as it was light that was all we could discover about our situation; but as soon as it got dark we noticed several other flame-coloured islands of various sizes in the vicinity, and far below us we could see a place full of towns and rivers and seas and forests and mountains, which we took to be the Earth.

We decided to do some more exploring, but we had not gone far before we were stopped and arrested by the local police. They are known in those parts as the Flying Squad, because they fly about on vultures, which they ride and control like horses. I should explain that the vultures in question are unusually large and generally have three heads. To give you some idea of their size, each of their feathers is considerably longer and thicker than the mast of a fairly large merchant-ship.

Now, one of the Flying Squad's duties is to fly about the country looking for undesirable aliens, and if it sees any to take them before the King. So that is what they did with us.

One glance at our clothes was enough to tell the King our nationality.

"Why, you're Greek, aren't you?" he said.

"Certainly we are," I replied.

"Then how on earth did you get here?" he asked. "How did you manage to come all that way through the air?"

So I told him the whole story, after which he told us his. It turned out that he came from Greece too, and was called Endymion. For some reason or other he had been whisked up here in his sleep and made King of the country, which was, he informed us, the Moon.

"But don't you worry," he went on. "I'll see you have everything you need. And if I win this war with Phaethon, you can settle down here quite comfortably for the rest of your lives."

"What's the war about?" I asked.

"Oh, it's been going on for ages," he answered. "Phaethon's my opposite number on the Sun, you know. It all started like this. I thought it would be a good idea to collect some of the poorer members of the community and send them off to form a colony on Lucifer, for it's completely uninhabited. Phaethon got jealous and despatched a contingent of airborne troops, mounted on flying ants, to intercept us when we were half-way there. We were hopelessly outnumbered and had to retreat, but now I'm going to have another shot at founding that colony, this time with full military support. If you'd care to join the expedition, I'd be only too glad to supply you with vultures from the royal stables, and all other necessary equipment. We start first thing tomorrow morning."

"Thanks very much," I said. "We'd love to come."

So he gave us an excellent meal and put us up for the night, and early next morning assembled all his troops in battle-formation, for the enemy were reported to be not far off. The expeditionary force numbered a hundred thousand, exclusive of transport, engineers, infantry, and foreign auxiliaries, eighty thousand being mounted on vultures, and the other twenty on saladfowls. Saladfowls, incidentally, are like very large birds, except that they are fledged with vegetables instead of feathers and have wings composed of enormous lettuce-leaves.

The main force was supported by a battery of Peashooters and a corps of Garlic-gassers, and also by a large contingent of allies from the Great Bear, consisting of thirty thousand Flea-shooters and fifty thousand Wind-jammers. Flea-shooters are archers mounted on fleas—hence their name—the fleas in question being approximately twelve times the size of elephants. Wind-jammers are also airborne troops, but they are not mounted on anything, nor do they have any wings of their own. Their method of propulsion is as follows: they wear extremely long night-shirts, which belly out like sails in the wind and send them scudding along like miniature ships through the air. Needless to say, their equipment is usually very light.

In addition to all these, seventy thousand Sparrow-balls and fifty thousand Crane Cavalry were supposed to be arriving from the stars that shine over Cappadocia, but I did not see any of them, for they never turned up. In the circumstances I shall not attempt to describe what they were like—though I heard some stories about them which were really quite incredible.

All Endymion's troops wore the same type of equipment. Their helmets were made of beans, which grow very large and tough up there, and their bodies

were protected by lupine seed-pods, stitched together to form a sort of armour-plate; for on the Moon these pods are composed of a horny substance which is practically impenetrable. As for their shields and swords, they were of the normal Greek pattern.

Our battle-formation was as follows. On the right wing were the troops mounted on vultures; among them was the King, surrounded by the pick of his fighting men, which included us. On the left wing were the troops mounted on saladfowls, and in the centre were the various allied contingents.

The infantry numbered approximately sixty million, and special steps had to be taken before they could be suitably deployed. There are, you must understand, large numbers of spiders on the Moon, each considerably larger than the average island in the Archipelago, and their services were requisitioned to construct a continuous cobweb between the Moon and Lucifer. As soon as the job had been done and the infantry had thus been placed on a firm footing, Nycterion, the third son of Eudianax, led them out on to the field of battle.

On the enemy's left wing was stationed the Royal Ant Force, with Phaethon himself among them. These creatures looked exactly like ordinary flying ants, except for their enormous size, being anything up to two hundred feet long. They carried armed men on their backs, but with their huge antennae they did just as much of the fighting as their riders. They were believed to number about fifty thousand.

On the right wing were placed an equal number of Gnat-shooters, who were archers mounted on giant gnats. Behind them was a body of mercenaries from outer space. These were only light-armed infantry, but were very effective long-range fighters, for they bombarded us with colossal radishes, which inflicted foul-smelling wounds and caused instantaneous death. The explanation was said to be that the projectiles were smeared with a powerful antiseptic.

Next to the mercenaries were about ten thousand Mushroom Commandos, heavy-armed troops trained for hand-to-hand fighting who used mushrooms as shields and asparagus stalks as spears; and next to them again were five thousand Bow-wows from Sirius. These were dog-faced human beings mounted on flying chestnuts.

It was reported that Phaethon too had been let down by some of his allies, for an army of slingers was supposed to be coming from the Milky Way, and the Cloud-Centaurs had also promised their support. But the latter arrived too late for the battle (though far too soon for my comfort, I may add) and the slingers never turned up at all. Phaethon, I heard, was so cross about it that he went and burnt their milk for them shortly afterwards.

Eventually the signal-flags went up, there was a loud braying of donkeys on both sides—for donkeys are employed as trumpeters up there—and the battle began. The enemy's left wing immediately turned tail and fled, long before our vulture-riders had got anywhere near them, so we set off in pursuit and killed as many as we could. Their right wing, however, managed to break through our left one, and the Gnat-shooters came pouring through the gap until they were stopped by our infantry, who promptly made a counter-attack and forced them to retreat. Finally, when they realised that their left wing had already been beaten, the retreat became an absolute rout. We took vast numbers of prisoners, and killed so many men that the blood splashed all over the clouds and made them as red as a sunset. Quite a lot of it dripped right down on to the earth, and made me wonder if something of the sort had happened before, which would account for that extraordinary statement in Homer that Zeus rained down tears of blood at the thought of Sarpedon's death.

In the end we got tired of chasing them, so we stopped and erected two trophies, one in the middle of the cobweb to commemorate the prowess of the infantry, and one in the clouds to mark the success of our airborne forces. Just as we were doing so, a report came through that Phaethon's unpunctual allies, the Cloud-Centaurs, were rapidly approaching. When they finally appeared they were a most astonishing sight, for they were a cross between winged horses and human beings. The human part was about as big as the Colossus at Rhodes, and the horse-part was roughly the size of a large merchant-ship. I had better not tell you how many there were of them, for you would never believe me, if I did, but you may as well know that they were led by Sagittarius, the archer in the Zodiac.

Hearing that their allies had been defeated, they sent a message to Phaethon telling him to rally his forces and make a counter-attack. In the meantime they set the example by promptly spreading out in line and charging the Moon-people before they had time to organise themselves—for they had broken ranks as soon as the rout began, and now they were scattered about all over the place in search of loot. The result was that our entire army was put to flight, the King himself was chased all the way back to his capital, and most of his birds lost their lives.

The Cloud-Centaurs pulled down the trophies and devastated the whole cobweb, capturing me and two of my friends in the process. By this time

Phaethon had returned to the scene of action and erected some trophies of his own, after which we were carried off to the Sun as prisoners of war, our hands securely lashed behind our backs with pieces of cobweb.

The victors decided not to besiege Endymion's capital, but merely to cut off his light-supply by building a wall in the middle of the air. The wall in question was composed of a double thickness of cloud, and was so effective that the Moon was totally eclipsed and condemned to a permanent state of darkness. Eventually Endymion was reduced to a policy of appeasement, and sent a message to Phaethon, humbly begging him to take down the wall and not make them spend the rest of their lives in the dark, volunteering to pay a war-indemnity and conclude a pact of non-aggression with the Sun, and offering hostages as a guarantee of his good faith.

Phaethon's Parliament met twice to consider these proposals. At the first meeting they passed a res-

olution rejecting them out of hand; at the second they
reversed this decision, and agreed to make peace on
terms which were ultimately incorporated in the following document:

AN AGREEMENT made this day between
the Sun-people and their allies (hereinafter
called *The Victors*) of the one part and the
Moon-people and their allies (hereinafter
called *The Vanquished*) of the other part
1. The Victors agree to demolish the wall, to
refrain in future from invading the Moon, and
to return their prisoners of war at a fixed charge
per head.
2. The Vanquished agree not to violate the sov-
ereign rights of other stars, and not to make war
in future upon the Victors, but to assist them in
case of attack by a third party, such assistance to
be reciprocal.

3. The Vanquished undertake to pay to the Victors annually in advance ten thousand bottles of dew, and to commit ten thousand hostages to their keeping.

4. The colony on Lucifer shall be established jointly by both parties, other stars being free to participate if they so wish.

5. The terms of this agreement shall be inscribed on a column of amber, to be erected in the middle of the air on the frontier between the two kingdoms.

SIGNED for and on behalf of
the Sun-people and their allies
RUFAS T. FIREMAN
for and on behalf of the
Moon-people and their allies
P. M. LOONY

As soon as peace was declared, the wall was taken down and we three prisoners were released. When we got back to the Moon, we were greeted with tears of joy not only by the rest of our party but

even by Endymion himself. He was very anxious for me to stay and help him with the colony, and actually offered to let me marry his son—for there are no such things as women on the Moon—but I was intent on getting down to the sea again, and as soon as he realised that I had made up my mind, he gave up trying to keep me. So off we went, after a farewell dinner which lasted for a week.

At this point I should like to tell you some of the odd things I noticed during my stay on the Moon. First of all, their methods of reproduction: as they have never even heard of women up there, the men just marry other men, and these other men have the babies. The system is that up to the age of twenty-five one acts as a wife, and from then on as a husband.

When a man is pregnant, he carries the child not in his stomach but in the calf of his leg, which grows extremely fat on these occasions. In due course they do a Caesarean, and the baby is taken out dead; but it is then brought to life by being placed in a high wind with its mouth wide open. Incidentally, it seems to me that these curious facts of lunar physiology may throw some light on a problem of etymology, for have we not here the missing link between the two apparently unconnected senses of the word *calf*?

Even more surprising is the method of propagating what are known as Tree-men. This is how it is done: you cut off the father's right testicle and plant it in the ground, where it grows into a large fleshy tree rather like a phallus, except that it has leaves and branches and bears fruit in the form of acorns, which are about eighteen inches long. When the fruit is ripe, it is picked and the babies inside are hatched out.

It is not uncommon up there to have artificial private parts, which apparently work quite well. If you are rich, you have them made of ivory, but the poorer classes have to rub along with wooden ones.

When Moon-people grow old, they do not die. They just vanish into thin air, like smoke—and talking of smoke, I must tell you about their diet, which is precisely the same for everyone. When they feel hungry, they light a fire and roast some frogs on it—for there are lots of these creatures flying about in the air. Then, while the frogs are roasting, they draw up chairs round the fire, as if it were a sort of dining-room table, and gobble up the smoke.

That is all they ever eat, and to quench their thirst they just squeeze some air into a glass and drink that: the liquid produced is rather like dew. They never make water in the other sense, nor do they ever evacuate their bowels, having no hole in that part of their anatomy; and if this makes you wonder what they do with their wives, the answer is that they have a hole in the crook of the knee, conveniently situated immediately above the calf.

Bald men are considered very handsome on the Moon, and long hair is thought absolutely revolting; but on young stars like the comets, which have not yet lost their hair, it is just the other way round—or so at least I was told by a Comet-dweller who was having a holiday on the Moon when I was there.

I forgot to mention that they wear their beards a little above the knee; and they have not any toe-nails, for the very good reason that they have not any toes. What they have got, however, is a large cabbage growing just above the buttocks like a tail. It is always in flower, and never gets broken, even if they fall flat on their backs.

When they blow their noses, what comes out is extremely sour honey, and when they have been working hard or taking strenuous exercise, they sweat milk at every pore. Occasionally they turn it into cheese, by adding a few drops of the honey. They also make olive-oil out of onions, and the resulting fluid is extremely rich and has a very delicate perfume.

They have any number of vines, which produce not wine but water, for the grapes are made of ice; and there, in my view, you have the scientific explanation of hail-storms, which occur whenever the wind is strong enough to blow the fruit off those vines.

They use their stomachs as handbags for carrying things around in, for they can open and shut them at will. If you look inside one, there is nothing to be seen in the way of digestive organs, but the whole interior is lined with fur so that it can also be used as a centrally-heated pram for babies in cold weather.

The upper classes wear clothes made of flexible glass, but this material is rather expensive, so most people have to be content with copper textiles—for there is any amount of copper in the soil, which becomes as soft as wool when soaked in water.

I hardly like to tell you about their eyes, for fear you should think I am exaggerating, because it really does sound almost incredible. Still, I might as well risk it, so here goes: their eyes are detachable, so that you can take them out when you do not want to see anything and put them back when you do. Needless to say, it is not unusual to find someone who has mislaid his own eyes altogether and is always having to borrow someone else's; and those who can afford it keep quite a number of spare pairs by them, just in case. As for ears, the Tree-men have wooden ones of their own, and everyone else has to be satisfied with a couple of plane-tree leaves instead.

I must just mention one other thing that I saw in the King's palace. It was a large mirror suspended over a fairly shallow tank. If you got into the tank, you could hear everything that was being said on the Earth, and if you looked in the mirror, you could see what was going on anywhere in the world, as clearly as if you were actually there yourself. I had a look at all the people I knew at home, but whether they saw me or not, I really cannot say.

Well, that is what it was like on the Moon. If you do not believe me, go and see for yourself.

—*Translated by Paul Turner*

BARON MUNCHAUSEN

A Second Trip to the Moon

SECOND VISIT (but an accidental one) to the moon. The ship driven by a whirlwind a thousand leagues above the surface of the water, where a new atmosphere meets them and carries them into a capacious harbour in the moon. A description of the inhabitants, and their manner of coming into the lunarian world. Animals, customs, weapons of war, wine, vegetables, etc.

I HAVE ALREADY informed you of one trip I made to the moon, in search of my silver hatchet; I afterwards made another in a much pleasanter manner, and stayed in it long enough to take notice of several things, which I will endeavour to describe as accurately as my memory will permit.

I went on a voyage of discovery at the request of a distant relation, who had a strange notion that there were people to be found equal in magnitude to those described by Gulliver in the empire of BROBDIG-NAG. For my part I always treated that account as fabulous: however, to oblige him, for he had made me his heir, I undertook it, and sailed for the South Seas, where we arrived without meeting with anything remarkable, except some flying men and women who were playing at leap-frog, and dancing minuets in the air.

On the eighteenth day after we had passed the Island of Otaheite, mentioned by Captain Cook as the place from whence they brought Omai, a hurricane blew our ship at least one thousand leagues above the surface of the water, and kept it at that height till a fresh gale arising filled the sails in every part, and onwards we travelled at a prodigious rate; thus we proceeded above the clouds for six weeks. At last we discovered a great land in the sky, like a shining island, round and bright, where, coming into a convenient harbour, we went on shore, and soon found it was inhabited. Below us we saw another earth, containing cities, trees, mountains, rivers, seas, etc., which we

conjectured was this world which we had left. Here we saw huge figures riding upon vultures of a prodigious size, and each of them having three heads. To form some idea of the magnitude of these birds, I must inform you that each of their wings is as wide and six times the length of the main sheet of our vessel, which was about six hundred tons burthen. Thus, instead of

riding upon horses, as we do in this world, the inhabitants of the moon (for we now found we were in
Madam Luna) fly about on these birds. The king, we
found, was engaged in a war with the sun, and he
offered me a commission, but I declined the honour
his majesty intended me. Everything in *this* world is of
extraordinary magnitude! a common flea being much
larger than one of our sheep: in making war, their
principal weapons are radishes, which are used as
darts: those who are wounded by them die immediately. Their shields are made of mushrooms, and their
darts (when radishes are out of season) of the tops of
asparagus. Some of the natives of the dog-star are to be
seen here; commerce tempts them to ramble; their
faces are like large mastiffs', with their eyes near the
lower end or tip of their noses: they have no eyelids,
but cover their eyes with the end of their tongues
when they go to sleep; they are generally twenty feet
high. As to the natives of the moon, none of them are

less in stature than thirty-six feet: they are not called the human species, but the cooking animals, for they all dress their food by fire, as we do, but lose no time at their meals, as they open their left side, and place the whole quantity at once in their stomach, then shut it again till the same day in the next month; for they never indulge themselves with food more than twelve times a year, or once a month. All but gluttons and epicures prefer this method to ours.

There is but one sex either of the cooking or any other animals in the moon; they are all produced from trees of various sizes and foliage; that which produces the cooking animal, or human species, is much more beautiful than any of the others; it has large straight boughs and flesh-coloured leaves, and the fruit it produces are nuts or pods, with hard shells at least two yards long; when they become ripe, which is known from their changing color, they are gathered with great care, and laid by as long as they think proper: when they choose to animate the seed of these nuts, they throw them into a large cauldron of boiling water, which opens the shells in a few hours, and out jumps the creature.

Nature forms their minds for different pursuits before they come into the world; from one shell comes forth a warrior, from another a philosopher, from a third a divine, from a fourth a lawyer, from a fifth a farmer, from a sixth a clown, etc., etc., and each of them immediately begins to perfect themselves, by practising what they before knew only in theory.

When they grow old they do not die, but turn into air, and dissolve like smoke! As for their drink, they need none; the only evacuations they have are insensible, and by their breath. They have but one finger upon each hand, with which they perform everything in as perfect a manner as we do who have four besides the thumb. Their heads are placed under their right arm, and when they are going to travel, or about any violent exercise, they generally leave them at home, for they can consult them at any distance; this is a very common prac- tice; and when those of rank or quality among the Lunarians have an inclination to see what's going forward among the common people, they stay at home, *i.e.*, the body stays at home, and sends the head only, which is suffering to be present *incog.*, and returns at pleasure with an account of what has passed.

The stones of their grapes are exactly like hail; and I am perfectly satisfied that when a storm or high wind in the moon shakes their vines, and breaks the grapes from the stalks, the stones fall down and form our hail showers. I would advise those who are of my opinion to save a quantity of these stones when it hails next, and make Lunarian wine. It is a common beverage at St. Luke's. Some material circumstances I had nearly omitted. They put their bellies to the same use as we do a sack, and throw whatever they have occasion for into it, for they can shut and open it again when they please, as they do their stomachs; they are not troubled with bowels, liver, heart, or any other intestines, neither are they encumbered with clothes, nor is there any part of their bodies unseemly or indecent to exhibit.

Their eyes they can take in and out of their places when they please, and can see as well with them in their hand as in their head! and if by any accident they lose or damage one, they can borrow or purchase another, and see as clearly with it as their own. Dealers in eyes are on that account very numerous in most parts of the moon, and in this article alone all the inhabitants are whimsical: sometimes green and sometimes yellow eyes are the fashion. I know these things appear strange; but if the shadow of a doubt can remain on any person's mind, I say, let him take a voyage there himself, and then he will know I am a traveller of veracity.

ILLUSTRATIONS

AUTHORS

E. E. CUMMINGS was known primarily for his experiments with form and structure in poetry. This poem, entitled "who knows" is from *Complete Poems 1904-1962*.

German astronomer JOHANN KEPLER first established the law of planetary motion, i.e., that the planets move in elliptical orbit around the sun. His 1595 *Somnium* is the classic imaginary journey to the moon. The book was not published until after Kepler's death, as a work of such silliness would have destroyed his scientific reputation.

H. G. WELLS' literary output is vast, but he is best known for his scientific romances, including *The War of the Worlds*, *The Time Machine*, and *The First Men in the Moon*. Wells died in 1946.

A famous soldier and duelist, CYRANO DE BERGERAC (1619-55) turned to writing after being wounded in the Spanish War. "Journey to the Moon" is from his fantastic *Other Worlds*.

The Greek writer LUCIAN OF SAMOSATA was famous for his satires. His masterpiece *True History* (c.125-200) influenced many more imaginary voyages, including Swift's *Gulliver's Travels*.

The Munchausen legends are built upon the grossly exaggerated exploits of the original BARON MUNCHAUSEN, a soldier said to have lived in 1720-97. These tales were popularized in English by Rudolph Erich Raspe.

ACKNOWLEDGMENTS

"Journey to the Moon" from *Other Worlds* by Cyrano de Bergerac ©1965 by Oxford University Press. Reprinted from *Other Worlds* by Cyrano de Bergerac translated by Geoffrey Strachen (1965) by permission of Oxford University Press.

"who knows if the moon's" by e. e. cummings reprinted from *Complete Poems 1904-1962*, by e. e. cummings, edited by George Firmage, by permission of Liveright Publishing Corporation. ©1923, 1925, 1951, 1953, 1991 by the Trustees for the e. e. cummings Trust ©1976 by George James Firmage.

Excerpt from *Somnium* from *Kepler's Dream, with Full Text and Notes of "Somnium, Sive Astronomia Lunaris"* reprinted by permission of University of California Press.

Excerpt from *The True History* by Lucian, translated by Paul Turner. Reprinted by permission of The Clader Educational Trust, London.